PTSD'S A BEAR

A Book for Everyone

ROBERT S. BROWN, MD, PHD

To Becky Templeman,
Thanks for being real;
not just a realtor!
Bob and Nannie B

8 September 2017

I dedicate this book to all the families of Soldiers

touched by War

Robert S. Brown, MD, PhD
COL, Medical Corps, USAR, (Ret.) Visiting Professor
Psychiatry and Neurobehavioral Sciences
School of Medicine
University of Virginia Charlottesville

ISBN: 9781520727226
Kindle Direct Publishing

Table of Contents

A LAZY SUMMER DAY

"I love the Fourth of July," said Tommy. "Next to Christmas, it's my favorite holiday."

The red-headed, freckle-faced 11-year-old, "going on 12," he always added, was lying comfortably on his back at the bottom, shady side, of a hill.

The "hill" in this part of Virginia is not very steep. The Appomattox River is at the bottom of this hill. It's a beautiful place to relax, and a great place to fish. Tommy discovered it, claimed it, and he keeps its location a secret.

Barefoot, an over-sized old white T-shirt, an even older pair of loose fitting blue jeans without a belt, and, oldest of all, straw hat was the comfortable way to dress for this rather thin, bony fisherman.

A string hung listlessly from the end of a yellow bamboo cane. This homemade fishing rod was held loosely in Tommy's right hand. On the far end of the line, a sharp hook firmly held a dangling earthworm, the bait that hungry fish loved.

Exactly three feet above the hook, a round, red and white-colored cork, shaped like a golf ball, but a little larger, supported the hook in the clear, fresh water.

On his second most favorite holiday, a hot one without a breeze, Tommy said, "Today, I'm going to catch a big catfish. You'll see.

No fish in this river can refuse the eight inch, red, juicy earthworm I dug up this morning in my back yard."

The bright, beautiful blue sky silently let the late summer sun to do its work.

A chemical plant down the river released smelly dark clouds. People got used to smelling. It lasted no longer than several hours, but it loomed over the area.

Little Bear is Tommy's fishing partner. Tommy and Little Bear have been friends since the first grade. Their strong friendship was so close that Tommy's mother, Betty, would often say, "If one of you boys took medication, the other one would have the side effects." Then she laughed.

Little Bear was already 12 years old. His brown hair and large, round, brown eyes helped form a pleasant, friendly face. Little Bear *liked* fishing, but he didn't *love* it; not like Tommy loved it. Given a choice, Little Bear would prefer reading. He had no line in the water today.

Little Bear's brown shoes, neatly pressed khaki pants with brown belt, and white dress shirt suggested he looked more like a nerd than a fisherman.

Friends Talk

"Fishing is okay," said Little Bear, "but there are other things to do, too."

"You're just jealous, Little Bear," said Tommy, "because I'm a better fisherman."

"I'm not jealous."

Little Bear did not like to argue. He had a temper; he got angry easily and then regretted what he had said in anger. He had heard other people say hurtful things, hard to forget things when they were angry. He didn't want to get mad and ruin his best friend's second most favorite holiday.

"You are better at fishing than I am. I'll give you that."

Tommy felt sorry for a moment. He too did not want to ruin a holiday.

"I'm sorry, Little Bear. I apologize for saying you're jealous. No hard feelings?"

"Of course I have no hard feelings."

No one spoke.

Tommy watched his cork in the water. He longed to see it bob up and down, followed by a powerful tug on his line. It would mean a big catfish had swallowed the hook and tried to swim away. Today the cork did not move. The bright sun's reflection off the water made it unpleasant, even painful, to watch the cork.

Tommy broke the silence. "Okay, I give up. It's just too hot for the fish to bite today. Let's go home. Maybe we should try again early tomorrow morning."

"You don't have to leave now because of what I said, Tommy. I'll stay as long as you like. Maybe I should not have said I'm going in an hour if the fish don't bite. I'm sorry I said that. I know you love fishing."

"It's okay," said Tommy. "I'm ready to go. We have a long, hot walk back home. Let's go."

Holidays

As the two best friends started to walk home, "Tommy," said Little Bear, "you said the Fourth of July is one of your two most favorite holidays."

"That's right. So what?"

"Do you know what we celebrate on the Fourth of July?"

"Stop it," he snapped.

"Stop what?"

"Stop talking school talk. I don't want to hear anything about school. We have exactly two more weeks of summer vacation before the first day of the school year begins. Please, Little Bear, no more school talk!"

"I never mentioned school, Tommy."

"That's where you were heading, Little Bear. You're getting ready to ask me questions that come up in school. Something about history or government is on your mind.

That stuff is not on my mind. I don't care about history when I'm on summer vacation. I don't want to hear about government when I'm on summer vacation.

Do you understand?"

Tommy's face was red. It was not red from the sun because his straw hat shielded his face from the sun. His face was red from anger.

Little Bear said nothing for the rest of the walk home. He did not lose his temper.

These two good friends lived on the same street, but, together they walked nearly every step in silence.

Little Bear reached his house first, and said, "See you, Tommy."

Tommy did not reply. It had been at least 15 minutes since he last spoke. His feelings were hurt, but he did not admit it.

There was no discussion of the meaning of the Fourth of July holiday.

There was no discussion of hurt feelings.

Something unusual was going to happen later. The importance of the Fourth of July was coming up again. Little Bear did not bring it up; it was someone else, someone they both liked very much.

Chloe

Tommy's twin sister, Chloe, is only 11 years old, but she seems much older because she is brilliant for her age. This red-headed somewhat smaller version of Tommy is also pushy and stubborn.

Tommy and Chloe are twins, but not friends. They don't hang out together. Tommy's friend is Little Bear. If Chloe has friends, they are books or librarians. The twins' strained relationship is a mystery and a disappointment to their mother, Betty. Someday, in a most unusual way, the mystery will be settled.

Chloe loves to read. Furthermore, she wants to talk about what she reads. Sometimes, even Tommy's mother can't answer all of Chloe's questions. When her questions remain unanswered, Chloe does not hide her disappointment.

When he returned home from fishing, Tommy was not in a good mood. He wanted to be left alone. There was a frown on Tommy's face. His morning fishing trip was a complete failure. Tommy wanted to sulk. Little Bear's friend wanted to sulk alone. He wanted to sulk in peace, but this was not going to be the case.

"Tommy," Chloe demanded, "walk with me to the library. I need some books to read."

Tommy shouted, "Get out of here and leave me alone!"

"I want to go now before all the right books are checked out!"

"I said get out of my room!"

"I want to read about The Fourth of July."

"Don't ever mention The Fourth of July to me again. I'm sick of it. It's a holiday. That's all you need to know. I mean it. Don't ever mention it to me again! Do you hear me? Scram!"

"I want to go to the library right this very minute. If you don't go with me, I will go alone."

"You know Mom does not like us to cross Main Street alone, *little girl*." "You may have been born 5 minutes before me, but I'm far more mature that you will ever be," Chloe said. "Never, and I mean it, never call me "*little girl*" again!"

Tommy shouted, "Mom, Chloe needs you!"

"There's no reason to call for mom. She left in the car, just as you walked in the house. Check the note she left. You are to "look out" for me until she returns.

"Have a nice day. I'm off to the library," Chloe said.

Tommy quickly read the note. Chloe was correct, but she was also on her way to the library, and she went alone.

Tommy was breathless when he finally caught up with Chloe, two blocks from the house. She had not yet reached Main Street, but she would have crossed it alone.

Together, two stubborn, red-headed children, one 11, the other 5 minutes younger, brother and sister, one holding the other's hand, the other's hand trying to pull away, were briskly walking to the Colonial Heights Public Library on a hot day in July.

Two things annoyed Tommy. He caught no fish, and his best friend ruined one of his favorite holidays. He did not believe it was possible, but his bad day will soon get worse.

2

DOROTHY ANN

Tommy finished all his chores by early afternoon. He completed his sulking, and he accomplished his unplanned library trip. His mother resumed her role as a parent to Chloe. He felt relieved.

At last, Tommy was fully into his favorite thing. His favorite thing at this time was nothing. Yes, that's correct. There were times when Tommy loved "doing nothing."

Little Bear's phone rang.

"Little Bear," said Tommy, "I'm calling to see if you want to get together this afternoon."

"Sure," said Little Bear. "What's on your mind?"

"Nothing, I just thought we could meet at the Mall, and, you know, do nothing. What do you say to that?"

"I'm up for doing nothing. What time you want to meet?"

"Now works for me."

In 15 minutes, the friends met and did nothing. They were happy. Doing nothing was fun. It seemed like they never had a disagreement.

When she walked up, everything changed.

She was the prettiest girl in the 7th grade.

If the boys' hearts beat any faster, someone would have to call 911. In fact, they could use an Oxygen tank now, unless they soon stopped gasping for breath.

Photoshop was not needed to improve the appearance of Dorothy Ann.

One, she was a year older than the boys, and this meant everything to them.

Two, she greeted them, knew their names, and broke the code of the snooty upper-class students by speaking to them. They were elated.

Three, she was as lovely as Goldilocks. She was blond, fair, and like an angel. She was the girl who made the Three Bears famous. She made Tommy and Little Bear almost purr like cats just fed on cream.

Her sweet voice was like a hummingbird. You imagined it, more than heard it.

In a high pitched and lilting sweet voice, Goldilocks, also known as Dorothy Ann, said, "What a pleasant surprise. I was just thinking of both of you, not more than an hour ago."

"Really?" asked the boys in unison.

"Yes, I wondered what you were doing this summer, and I

14

need a big favor. Maybe it's too much to ask?"

Again, almost in unison, the boys replied, "No, nothing is too much. What is the favor?

We will do anything for you! Anything! Anything!

Please ask us."

A Big Favor for Dorothy Ann

"I don't know what to say. I had no idea that both of you would be so kind, and so eager to help me. I'm so grateful that I want to cry. I hoped you'd help, but I know you are busy with your lives. Why would you want to help me?"

"Dorothy Ann," Tommy stammered, "we've done nothing all summer. Helping you will give us something to do." He was very excited. It is fair to say that Tommy is often excited, but never like this.

Little Bear nodded his head, indicating he also wanted to help if he could. He was very calm. It would also be fair to say the Little Bear is quiet most of the time.

"Thank you, both. Thank you. Please call me Dottie. That's what my friends call me. Dottie Ann."

Little Bear said, "Dottie, how can we help you?"

It felt funny, like unusual, for Little Bear to call Dorothy Ann by any other name.

He said "Dottie" once, but could he say it again? He wondered. It was like speaking a foreign language. It just didn't feel right. For a moment, it even made his mouth feel different.

"Have you guys seen me recently?"

"No," said Tommy. "This is the first time we've seen you all summer. Have you been sick, Dottie? You don't look sick. You look beautiful."

"Thank you, Tommy.

"No, I have not been sick. I've been in summer school."

"Oh, no," said Tommy. "That must be horrible."

Little Bear said, "I'll bet you enjoyed it, Dottie."

"Little Bear, how did you know?"

"Because I know learning can be fun. I love to learn. My best friend has not yet discovered the joy of learning in school, have you, Tommy?"

Tommy felt ashamed in front of Dottie. His freckled face glowed red and hot from blushing. It was humiliating. It was painful, but it was true. He had not found the joy of learning.

"Tommy will love learning when he finds the right teacher," said Dottie with a reassuring smile.

Tommy felt better after Dottie's comment. Her smile was reassuring. He eagerly waited for her to request a favor.

"I missed three days of summer school because I went to the beach with my parents. Now I'm behind. I must write a 5-page paper by tomorrow morning."

"What's the topic?" inquired Little Bear.

"The reason we celebrate the Fourth of July," said Dottie Ann.

Tommy's hope to help rescue Dottie sank suddenly like a torpedoed ship. Under his breath, he said, "O no; now she will never like me."

Little Bear becomes a Hero

"Let's go to the library and check out some books about the Fourth of July," said Tommy. He wanted to impress Dottie. If he did impress her, it was only for a brief moment because Little Bear innocently ruined it.

It came as a surprise, but Tommy was about to be shamed again in front of Dottie.

Little Bear spoke with confidence. "It's too late for the library, Tommy, but it's not too late for what Dottie has in her book bag."

"How do you know what's in her book bag?" demanded Tommy. His loud voice and red face showed he was very annoyed.

"I know that informed people are connected. In the Age of Information, bright people keep devices within easy reach; devices plugged into the ethernet. Dottie is informed and bright. Dottie probably has an iPad in her book bag."

"Little Bear, you are a genius. Why didn't I think of that?"

"You are too upset about the result of not meeting the deadline. You must write your paper by tomorrow morning.

There are some tables and chairs in front of the Barnes and Noble Book Store. Let's sit over there. We can probably pick up their Wi-Fi."

With Dottie's Apple iPad in his hands, Little Bear led Dottie and Tommy to a comfortable table. It worked. He was in charge. He was doing a good job while doing a good deed.

Poor Tommy. Now it's too late. "Why didn't I let Little Bear talk to me this morning about the Fourth of July?" he thought with grave regret.

Tommy saw it. The way Dottie looked at Little Bear solving her summer school problem was a look he never got from her. It was a unique look. It hurt Tommy's feelings deeply.

"It was too late." Tommy could not get the idea out of his mind that it was simply too late for Dottie to care for him as she cares for Little Bear.

"Let's get it done now," said Little Bear. "Let's write your paper."

"No," said Dottie. "You can't write my paper for me. That would not be honest. I must write it myself."

"I understand," said Little Bear, "we will search the topic online." Seeing that his friend felt left out, Little Bear added, "We will read some of the search results out loud. All three of us can discuss the results, and we can make an outline. If you like it, then you can use the outline to help you write your paper later."

Tommy liked the idea. Dottie adored the idea. The search began.

What we celebrate on the Fourth of July was a good search topic. An hour passed in a flash. The discussion was rich. Two Virginia State University students stopped by, listened for a moment, and then shook their heads in amazement.

"Let's make the outline for Dottie's paper a work of art," said Little Bear.

Dottie was just a little uncertain. She needed Little Bear to explain his phrase, "a work of art." "Are we going to use colors and draw pictures?" she asked.

"No, Dottie. In this case, a "work of art" is a "thing of

beauty." The truth is beautiful. Your paper will be a "thing of beauty" because it will be entirely truthful."

Nearly swooning, Dottie said, "Little Bear, I did not know until today just how much you understand. That is awesome. You are awesome." She held up her hand to make the "V" sign for victory.

Tommy was in pain, the pain that only jealousy can create. Tommy was learning at last, however, that learning can impress girls. Silently, he decided he would never give up an opportunity to learn, even if was during summer break.

Little Bear was ill at ease by the kind things Dottie was saying about him. He did not want his friend to feel left out.

Little Bear said, "We have found some hot stuff on Google. I notice that Tommy was really into the things we discussed. Let me ask Tommy what he thinks we celebrate on the Fourth of July."

"Freedom," said Tommy. "And we celebrate our independence."

"Good, Tommy. Freedom from what?"

"In 1776, it was freedom from Great Britain, but today it is freedom from any oppression."

"Great, Tommy.

"Dottie, what else do we celebrate?"

"We also celebrate the freedom from any government, including our government, if it does anything more than secure our rights."

"Excellent. Superb," said Little Bear.

"Anybody, how did we make this clear?"

Tommy shouted, "We declared our independence from Great Britain on the Fourth of July, 1776. Everybody knows that."

"I wish you were correct, Tommy. Sadly, too many of our citizens do not know it."

"And soon after that, we wrote it in our constitution," shouted Dottie.

"You two do not have to yell. The managers may ask us to leave Barnes and Noble if we make a scene out here on the sidewalk.

We almost have our outline for Dottie's summer school paper.

How did we win our independence? Was it just given to us because we said we wanted it?"

"No," said Dottie. "We had to form an army and fight for it."

"Who was the first person to lead our military?" asked Little Bear.

"Thomas Jefferson," said Tommy.

"No, no, no, Tommy. You of all people should know that it was George Washington. Ask your father. He's a Soldier. He knows the history of the U.S. Army.

Last question: why do we have to keep a strong army?"

Dottie said, "It makes me sad to answer your question because the enemy killed my grandfather in World War II, and a rocket injured my uncle in the Global War on Terror."

Suddenly, the three happy young people changed from a glad to a sad mood.

Tommy said, "Our freedom is not free. Now I know what that means."

"Yes," Dottie said, "but we must keep a strong army to protect our freedom."

Special thanks

"Thank both of you for helping me today. I honestly never put these important thoughts together before," said Dottie.

"I never thought about the courage it took for a new, small nation to stand up to a giant like Great Britain in 1776, the strongest nation in the world at that time.

I never thought about how important it is to be free.

I never thought about the fact that our government doesn't give us our rights. God gives us our rights.

I never appreciated how important our nation considered God.

If I ever knew that God was given the most prominent place in our Declaration of Independence, I had forgotten it. It makes me want to learn more about God."

Tommy said, his confidence feeling somewhat restored, "Dottie, I would like to find out more about God, too. I don't know why God gives our rights. Can we all get together like this and study about the importance of God?"

"That's a fantastic idea, Tommy. I'm so pleased that you thought of it. God gives us our rights because He loves us. We did not earn them; God created us, knows what we need, and God provides us with everything we need.

Yes, let's make plans to get together again right here one week from today. Summer school will be over. I will have more time. That works for me. I'll bring my Bible."

Tommy had a warm feeling inside. No longer ashamed or annoyed, Tommy felt good. Dottie gave him a real compliment. It was not the same feeling he got from fishing, but it was just as good. Maybe, it was even better.

Dottie continued to express her thoughts about the U.S. Constitution. "It states plainly that our rights to life, liberty, and the pursuit of happiness come from God.

Our government's most essential task is to assure our rights."

Dottie stood up, put her iPad in her book bag, and very lightly, in the spirit of deep friendship and gratitude, kissed each of her friends on the cheek, and left.

Tommy and Little Bear, touched and surprised by Dottie's soft kiss, could not move.   Her kiss emotionally glued them to their seats.

It was as if they could not move or speak.

Time stopped.

It was a powerful combination of divine insight into the beginning of America, and how good it felt to be with Dottie.

Tommy said, as they got up to leave, "I'll never wash my face again."

Little Bear said, "Tommy, my best friend, do you have a Bible?"

"Sure; everybody has a Bible in their house. If we don't have one, I will ask my mother to buy one."

"Good, Tommy. Ask your mother to find a study Bible, one with footnotes that help explain the verses. That's the kind we have. When dad is home, we read it together every night as a family.

You know something? I bet Chloe has one and she can tell you how to find the best version of the study Bible."

"Don't worry, Little Bear. When we meet here next week, I will bring a Bible and my computer. We can connect to Bible Hub online. It's a great place for helping understand the Bible."

Contented and pleased, the two friends slowly walked home together. They didn't talk much, but they didn't have to.

3

CHLOE ASKS QUESTIONS

It was bedtime, but Chloe never liked going to bed.

Tommy was quietly reading a small book on fly fishing.

Betty was folding laundry.

Chloe said, "Who can tell me about Goldilocks and the Three Bears?"

"Not that again, Chloe. You are obsessed with the Three Bears. Please don't start that up again. What's wrong with you, girl? It's not cool."

"Tommy," said Betty, "do not speak to your sister that way."

"What way?"

"You are rude. There is never an excuse for rudeness."

"I can't take it, Mom. Chloe always talks about the Three Bears. Why does she do it? Why is an 11-year-old girl, almost twelve, interested in fairy tales?"

"Ask her."

"Chloe, please tell me why the Three Bears are so important to you."

"If you would like to know, Tommy, I will tell you.

Sometimes, I think of us as the Three Bears. We are not a mother, father, and a baby bear, but we are like a family of a mother, brother, and a twin sister bear."

"Mother, Chloe is silly, and I don't like it."

"Let her finish her explanation, Tommy. You told me that you wanted to start learning about things. You are learning how much fun it is to learn. We can learn a lot by listening.

It may surprise you to hear to what your sister thinks about the Three Bears."

Chloe turned to her mother and said, "Mother, does Tommy want to know why I reflect on the Three Bears?"

"Yes, darling, but Tommy doesn't know why they are on your mind so often. Maybe he'll have some answers to the questions you ask me about them."

It was unusual to see such an excellent, such an able, and such a cute young person describe her knowledge of and her serious interest in a fairy tale written long ago.

Chloe spoke earnestly about the Three Bears.

Who was Goldilocks?

Chloe answered her question.

"Goldilocks was the girl whose hair was the color of gold. Her eyes were as blue as the sky. Goldilocks was beautiful.

The fairytale does not tell us Goldilocks' age. I guess that Goldilocks was eleven or nearly twelve years old.

Whatever Goldilocks did, she was not happy until it was "just right."

She did not eat the Three Bears' porridge if it was too hot or too cold. It had to be "just right."

She did not sit in a chair if it was too small or too big. It had to be "just right."

Goldilocks did not rest in a bed that was too hard or too soft. It had to be "just right," Chloe explained.

"The story does not tell us why Goldilocks had to have everything "just right.""

Tommy did not interrupt. He listened. Curiously, Tommy had never focused on Goldilocks's need to have things "just right." He wanted to hear more.

Who were the Three Bears?

Chloe could tell she had her brother's attention, so she continued speaking.

"The Three Bears were a family.

Before Goldilocks' visit, the Three Bears led a quiet, peaceful life.

The Three Bears lived in a small, safe house in the woods.

They treated each other with kindness, dignity, respect, and acceptance.

The Three Bears felt close to each other. They wanted the best for each other.

They told each other what was happening in their life. They were friendly to each other. They liked each other. They liked to be with each other.

The Three Bears loved each other, just like we do," said Chloe.

"Goldilocks went for a walk in the forest. She came to the home of the Three Bears.

No one was at home, but Goldilocks went into their home, anyway.

Goldilocks ate the Three Bears' porridge. Today, we call porridge "oatmeal."

She sat in their chairs and broke two of them. It was an accident, but it did not stop Goldilocks. She persisted on her adventure.

The same thing happened to the Three Bears' beds. Goldilocks accidentally broke them.

Goldilocks acted as if it were her home. She did whatever she wanted.

When the Three Bears returned home, they found Goldilocks asleep in Baby Bear's bed.

When Goldilocks awakened, she was frightened by the Three Bears.

Goldilocks ran out of the Three Bears' home.

She ran out of the home into the forest. Goldilocks never returned to the Three Bears' home. I wonder what happened to the three bears after Goldilocks."

Goldilocks was Gone but Not Forgotten

"Goldilocks was gone, but this is what I think happened to the Three Bears after the story ends?"

"Wait just a minute. Are you making up a different end to the Three Bears?" asked Tommy.

"Yes."

Tommy shook his head in shock. "Mom, Chloe can't write a new ending to a story written long ago. Can she?"

"I did no write anything," said Chloe. "That might be wrong. It might look like I am stealing someone's work.

31

It's just something in my mind. It's not written down or anything like that."

Chloe made her point. Tommy did not like it, but he did not know what to say.

Chloe continued. Speaking seriously, she said, "Mama and Papa Bear were unhappy. Mama Bear said, "If Goldilocks knocked on our door, I would have welcomed her, but she came inside when we were not home. Goldilocks did not obey the law.

I do not like anyone in my home when I am not here."

Papa Bear said, "I feel the same way you do about our home."

The Three Bears cleaned up the mess Goldilocks left.

Papa Bear repaired the broken chairs and the broken beds.

Mama Bear put the empty breakfast bowls in the dishwasher.

Baby Bear said he could not understand why a stranger wanted to mess up their house."

Strangers

Chloe spoke earnestly, believing every word she reported from her excellent account of the Three Bears' new ending.

"Let this be a lesson to you, Baby Bear," said Mama Bear. "Always stay away from people you don't know. You can never tell what a stranger might do."

"You don't have to worry about me," said Baby Bear. "I know who's a friendly stranger and who's an evil stranger."

"Just a minute," said Mama Bear. "Repeat what you just said. I want Papa Bear to hear it."

Papa Bear wiped the sweat from his face. He had been working hard fixing the furniture Goldilocks broke during her unwelcome visit. He was tired. "What are you two talking about?" asked Papa Bear.

In a very firm voice, with a stern look on her face, Mama Bear said, "Baby Bear, tell Papa Bear what you just told me."

"I know the difference between a friendly stranger and an evil stranger," Baby Bear said proudly. "A kind stranger will give you a present."

Papa Bear made a growling sound. He did this when he was angry.

Mama Bear turned up her eyes. She shook her head. She was heartbroken with Baby Bear. She was furious with Baby Bear.

Mama Bear raised her voice. "Baby Bear," she said, "no

one can tell the difference between a friendly stranger and an evil stranger!

Papa Bear can't tell the difference.

I can't tell the difference," said Mama Bear.

"We are older than you. We have lived in the forest for a long time.

We can't tell the difference between good and bad strangers.

You can't tell the difference either, Baby Bear.

Get that thought out of your mind. That idea is not right.

It can be dangerous when you believe an idea is true when it is not true."

A Nice Stranger

"I thought she was a kind stranger because she gave me some honey," said Baby Bear.

"Who gave you honey?" Mama Bear demanded, more irritated now than ever.

"A few days ago, I was playing with the rabbits in the forest, and Goldilocks stopped to play with us," said Baby Bear.

"We liked her because she was pretty. She was also very

34

nice.

When I told her where we lived, she gave me some honey. She gave the rabbits some carrots," said Baby Bear. "She was very kind and friendly."

Mama Bear was steaming with anger. "I can't believe what I'm hearing," said Mama Bear." She walked up and down their small family room.

Why Goldilocks Visited the House of the Three Bears

"So now we know why Goldilocks came to our house.

It is your fault, Baby Bear.

You told a total stranger where we lived.

Tonight, you will go right to bed after supper! No TV. No video games!"

Papa Bear smiled. "It is not so bad, Mama Bear. I was able to fix everything Goldilocks broke."

Then Papa Bear turned to Baby Bear. "Son," he said, "this time talking to a stranger who gave you a gift turned out okay. Next time, we may not be so lucky.

Do you understand, Baby Bear?"

Baby Bear said, "Yes, Papa Bear."

Tommy was listening, and he was paying much attention

to all that Chloe said.

Baby Bear was Wrong

"Baby Bear felt real bad. He regretted talking to Goldilocks.

He was sorrowful. He had done wrong, but he learned not to do it again.

Now he knew it was wrong to take a gift from a stranger, even from a kind, lovely, friendly stranger.

"Momma and Papa," Baby Bear said. "I was wrong. I'm very sorry. I will never take a gift from a stranger again." Crying, Baby Bear walked slowly upstairs to his room.

"Baby Bear has learned his lesson, Mama Bear," said Papa Bear. "We don't have to be angry with him now or worried about this in the future."

"I hope and pray you are right," said Mama Bear.

Baby Bear's Dream

"As Baby Bear fell asleep that night, he was sad, but he soon filled his mind with his personal goal.

For as long as Baby Bear could remember, and to him, that seemed like a long time; he wanted to be a Soldier.

Baby Bear could see himself leading other Bears in the Army, defending his family and his forest.

He knew his thoughts would come true someday.

Baby Bear fell asleep with a little smile on his little face."

Tommy Responds

"I'm blown away," said Tommy. "Chloe, you must know more about the story of the Three Bears than anyone in the world!"

"They stay in my mind," said Chloe. "I have a big imagination; don't you, Tommy?"

"Not like yours. Not like yours," said Tommy, trying not to laugh at her.

"I don't think you are like Mother Bear in the story, Mother. You are never that mean.

I hardly remember dad, but I make-believe that dad was sort of like Papa Bear. In some ways, he was strong and caring."

Betty turned her head away to hide the tears in her eyes.

"Is there any more to your make-believe version of the famous story of Goldilocks and the Three Bears, Chloe?" asked Tommy.

"Yes," said an excited Chloe, the little girl who hates to go to bed. Chloe was pleased that her brother was showing an interest.

Chloe's worry

"I worry about what happened to the Three Bears after Goldilocks ran out of their house."

"Are you kidding me, genius?

"Goldilocks is not real! The Three Bears are not real!

Give us a break.

Which world do you live in? I mean, seriously. That is so uncool."

Betty said, "Tommy if you listen carefully, you can see how Chloe combines her two worlds."

"Mom, is that good? Can anyone live in two worlds at the same time? I mean?"

Chloe said, "I can, Tommy. I take characters from a story and see how they are like people I know. I can tell the difference, but sometimes I wish the people I know could be more like the people in the stories."

Tommy was speechless.

He looked at his mother. Tommy wanted more assurance that his sister was okay.

Betty said, "Tommy, Chloe is at the age where her

imagination is realistic and healthy. She also has no friends or playmates."

Betty hesitated, but then she said, "She has no father. A father is crucial to a girl her age, Tommy."

"I'm getting it now, mom." Shaking his head slowly, Tommy said, "I'm beginning to understand.

Go on, Chloe; take me to the end of this story.

Could you leave out some of the details? I'm getting sleepy.

Tell me the rest of your story as quickly as you can."

4

ONE MEANINGFUL NIGHT

Chloe continued her "factual" account of the Three Bears after Goldilocks, believing every word of it.

"On one special night, time galloped. Twenty years passed in one night.

All Three Bears were asleep.

When Baby Bear woke up the next morning, he had grown up.

Papa Bear woke up the next day. He was old enough to retire.

Mama Bear woke up as an older mother Bear. She liked shopping online.

Mama Bear also did volunteer work to help bears who did not have enough food to eat. She was an excellent seamstress. She made clothes for bears that were too poor to buy enough warm clothes for the winter.

And Baby Bear joined the Army."

SGT Bear

"Baby Bear came back from the Army as SGT Bear. He wore three stripes on the sleeve of his uniform.

SGT Bear brought home his wife, Lady Bear. She was very nice.

SGT Bear called his wife Lady Bear because she acted like a lady.

They called their baby, Little Bear. Little Bear was shy but bright.

The Three Bears were now Five Bears. The forest locals knew them as the Five Happy Bears.

The Five Bears had many friends in the woods. Some of their friends were devoted to them."

Tommy asks some Questions

"So, Chloe, if I understand your make-believe edition of the famous story of the Three Bears After Goldilocks, they lived happily ever after. Is that correct?"

"Yes."

"And you also think their story is like our story. Is that correct?"

"Yes."

"And each of the characters in the story reminds you of someone we all know?"

"Yes."

"Is there anyone else in our life today that you find in your story of The Three Bears after Goldilocks?"

"Yes."

"Chloe, please tell us who that person is?"

"Your friend, Little Bear."

"How in the world...?"

"Tommy," Betty said, "do not be rude. You have done fine up till now. Just let Chloe answer your question. You must both go to bed no later than a very a few minutes from now."

"Chloe, how does Little Bear fit into your story?"

"Little Bear *is* Little Bear in my story, The Three Bears after Goldilocks."

"You are either brilliant, or you are very crazy!"

"Tommy, apologize to your sister, right now," said Betty.

"I'm sorry. I apologize. I just never knew your mind worked this way. You have a fantastic and very odd imagination.

Little Bear's grandfather, Pastor Harold Bare, Covenant Church of God, Charlottesville, gave Little Bear his name.

Nobody knows Little Bear's real name, outside his family,

43

but me. It's Luther Bartholomew Bear.

As you know, he prefers to be called Little Bear. I guess SGT Bear is Big Bear in your story. Is that correct, Chloe?"

"No, in my story, SGT Bear is Baby Bear in the Three Bears."

The Painful Truth

"Guess who Goldilocks reminds me of the most?"

She hesitated, lowered her voice, and said, "Goldilocks tells me most of Daddy. He ran away, too, and we never heard from him again."

Betty leaped out of her chair and dashed out of the room. She was crying, touched by Chloe's tender thoughts about her dad.

Angrily, Tommy said, "Chloe, how can you say that? You know it upsets Mom to mention Dad."

Suddenly, Tommy stopped speaking.

Chloe was puzzled by Tommy's sudden change. "What's wrong, Tommy?"

Tommy spoke, but he did not look at Chloe. He was staring into space.

"Now I remember. I had forgotten, but Daddy never acted angry or self-centered around you. I never knew why, but that's the truth," he said seriously and softly.

Neither child spoke.

After a period of silence, Tommy asked how Chloe had learned about their Dad.

"I've talked to people who knew Daddy. He was a Soldier," Chloe said.

"The war changed Daddy.

I learned he had to have everything "just right." He yelled and stayed angry when things were not "just right," said Chloe.

"You don't know the half of it," said Tommy. "You don't know about the drinking, the nightmares, and the ways he kept all of us terrified.

You are right about Dad and Goldilocks. They both came into a house and broke it up. Yes, he had to have everything "just right," but "just right" was the way Dad defined it. It always had to be "just right" for him. It did not matter if it was not "just right" for us.

Sure, I miss him, too, but he never went for counseling."

Tommy cried. It hurt him to remember those miserable days and frightening nights.

Chloe had never seen her brother cry.

A Crucial day Ended

Something special happened that day. Tommy and Chloe felt closer to each other, closer than ever before. Betty could see it, and it pleased her.

Tommy no longer considered Chloe as a dumb twin sister. She was still stubborn, and she still had a strong will, but he respected her for trying to make sense of what had happened to their family. Most of all, he could see that Chloe believed that a happy ending for their family was still possible. It was something he had given up on long ago.

Chloe loved Tommy more because he was interested in what she thought.

Tommy discovered the love of learning, something that would direct his journey through the rest of his life.

Betty had a very profound sense of relief.

No one ever had to worry again about what happened to the Three Bears after Goldilocks. Chloe had reasoned it out. Not only had the Three Bears done well, but even the next generation of the Three Bears flourished.

Each member of this precious, caring family went to their bed that great night and slept in peace.

5

NEW SCHOOL YEAR

On the first day of the new school year, his teacher, Ms. Green, said, "Tommy, please stop talking. I trust you are happy to be back in school, but please stay in your seat, and please, Tommy, stop talking."

Summer break somehow makes students forget about school conduct.

When the class settled down, Ms. Green spoke again.

"Little Bear, tell us what makes you so happy today? I noticed you were smiling this morning, Little Bear."

"I didn't know I was smiling, but I feel happy and blessed. I feel thankful to be back in school," said Little Bear.

"Tell us what makes you feel so happy, blessed and thankful on the first day of school."

Little Bear gave the teacher's question a lot of thought.

Little Bear wanted his answers to be honest. He wanted to be truthful.

"I'm happy and thankful for my Mother.

I'm happy and thankful for my Grandparents.

I'm happy and grateful to live in a peaceful nation with my

family and friends."

My Dad is a Soldier

After thinking a few minutes more, Little Bear stood at attention like a Soldier.

Little Bear did what he had seen his dad do many times.

His back was straight.

His shoulders were squared.

He held his right hand to his forehead and smartly saluted.

"I'm happiest and most thankful that my Dad is a Soldier. He returned home safely from the fighting. My Dad helps protect us so we can live wherever we want to live."

Little Bear's classmates stood up and cheered.

"What is a Soldier, Little Bear?"

Ms. Green was Little Bear's sixth-grade teacher. She was a kind and caring person.

Ms. Green cared for the children she took care of, and she was a competent teacher.

Ms. Green wanted her class to learn about the world.

Today, Ms. Green wanted her class to learn about Soldiers.

She was happy to have the son of a Soldier in her class.

"What is a Soldier, Little Bear?" said Ms. Green.

"Tell the class what a Soldier is."

Little Bear's Definition of a Soldier

Little Bear was proud of his father, but he felt a little uneasy.

It was his first day of school this year. He knew only one of his classmates.

He could tell that his classmates wanted to learn about Soldiers by the way they got real quiet and stared at him. Their interest made him feel more anxious.

Little Bear could feel tiny drops of sweat forming on the palms of his hands. "I hope nobody can tell I'm nervous," he thought.

"I want to say the right things. I don't want to look stupid." These were two more thoughts Little Bear had.

"Little Bear," said Ms. Green, "we are waiting."

Hurriedly, Little Bear said, "A Soldier wears a uniform to work. He salutes people in uniform, and he stands up straight."

"Anything else?" asked Ms. Green.

"I don't know," said Little Bear.

"How can you find out?" asked Ms. Green.

"I can ask my dad," answered Little Bear.

Little Bear had a second thought. "I can ask my dad to come here to tell us what a Soldier is," he said.

Ms. Green said, "That is a good idea. Can your dad come to school tomorrow?"

"Yes, I believe dad can come to school tomorrow. Dad's on leave for thirty days. He is not real busy now."

The next day, SGT Bear and Little Bear came to school together.

Ms. Green and Little Bear's classmates were happy to meet SGT Bear.

SGT Bear brought Krispy Kreme doughnuts for the morning break.

When the class heard about their treat, they cheered.

"Little Bear," said Ms. Green, "please introduce your father to your classmates."

Little Bear was not anxious today. He felt secure whenever his dad was nearby.

Little Bear stood up and walked to the front of the class.

"Dad, will you please come up to the front?"

One of SGT Bear's Special Thoughts

SGT Bear stood up. He always felt good when Little Bear was nearby.

SGT Bear had a unique thought about Little Bear. "My young son is so innocent that it makes me feel good to be near him. He doesn't judge me."

SGT Bear had never told anyone about this particular thought. It was too precious to share.

Children don't know how important they are to their fathers.

Sometimes, it is not easy to be a good father.

Little Bear proudly introduced his father to his class. He said, "Classmates, meet my Dad, SGT Bear."

"Dad," said Little Bear, "meet my classmates and my teacher, Ms. Green."

Making certain that he included everyone, Little Bear smiled as he said, "Classmates, and Ms. Green, meet my Dad."

Everyone applauded loudly.

"Dad, before you start, please tell the class about your uniform. Tell us what each one of your medals stands for."

SGT Bear was not expecting Little Bear's question about

his medals and awards.

SGT Bear tended to be shy. He did not like to brag. He was afraid that talking about his medals would be bragging.

SGT Bear blushed. He pulled at the neck of his shirt, and for a moment he looked away from the students and stared at the floor.

Ms. Green sensed that SGT Bear suddenly felt uneasy.

Wanting to help, Ms. Green stood up and said, "SGT Bear, please tell us only what you think we need to know to understand what it means to be a Soldier."

SGT Bear Speaks

"Since the beginning of our country, we have needed Soldiers.

Soldiers make up our Army.

George Washington was the leader or commanding general of our first Army. Later, George Washington was elected the first president of the United States of America.

Our Soldiers protect and defend our nation against its enemies.

The uniform I wear today is called Dress Blues. The medals worn on my Dress Blues are symbols of things I had to do in combat.

Combat is fighting the enemies of this country.

Combat is also called "TIC" or Troops in Contact. Contact means armed contact with the enemy.

Troops refer to groups of Soldiers."

Explaining the War on Terror

SGT Bear wanted to tell Little Bear's class about something important.

He did not want to frighten them.

SGT Bear wanted the children to know that something bad happened to this country, but he wanted them to know that it was being amended, corrected, and put right. It was the reason we declared the Global War on Terror.

He wanted to tell the children. SGT Bear did not want to alarm them.

What he was going to tell the children is difficult to understand. It is not easy to explain. It is hard for everyone to figure out, even the wisest and most intelligent adults. It had never happened to us before this event.

Once upon a Time

SGT Bear looked around the room. The innocent faces of children gazed at him with keen interest.

"Once upon a time, not that long ago," SGT Bear said, "a dark cloud hung over a large section of the sky high above New York City. There never was a cloud like that cloud ever before in our nation's 200-year history." He pointed to the location of New York City on a large map of the US.

"We never want a cloud like that cloud ever again in our country.

The dark cloud formed on a beautiful, sun-filled, blue-sky day on September 11, 2001. It was not a dark cloud from bad weather. It was a black cloud from the actions of evil men.

All television channels showed the world what was happening.

First, an American airliner, filled with passengers, crashed into a very tall building in New York City.

In the beginning, most people thought it was a horrible accident, but that was not the truth.

In just a few minutes, a second passenger-filled airliner crashed into the adjacent building.

The two buildings, standing side by side, were called the Twin Towers. They were skyscrapers.

Thousands of people worked in the Twin Towers.

The nation could not believe what they saw on television

or heard on the radio.

When the second passenger-filled airliner crashed into the buildings, the buildings collapsed in explosions and fire.

People ran for their lives. Three thousand people did not make it to safety.

All the passengers in the airplanes were killed, including the evil men who took control of the planes and crashed them into the Twin Towers.

An evil man named Usama bin Laden boasted that he ordered the attacks on the United States' Twin Towers.

The United States' Response to the Attacks on our Nation

"No country in the world is as strong as America.

Weak states or evil men who hate our country cannot declare war on us. They lack the strength. They don't have enough military warriors. They resort to attacks or acts of terror.

Acts of terror are violent, unexpected, and intended to cause great fear and destruction.

The attack on the Twin Towers was an act of terror.

It was horrible. It was unthinkable. It was evil. It was terror."

Terror Cannot Defeat Us.

"Usama bin Laden worked with other evil men called the Al-Qaeda, a group that specializes in acts of terror.

Many of the evil men who commit acts of terror reside in the Middle East, a part of the world in which people have lived for thousands of years. Many of the problems for which terrorists attack each other are so old that the Bible tells us about them.

Usama bin Laden said he ordered the attack on America because we declared war on Muslims, a religious group whose history began in the 7th century. This is a lie.

Usama bin Laden kept lying; he said that we hate Muslims.

The United States hates no religion. The US hates no religious people.

This country is free. All individuals who live here are free. They are free to choose their religion. Everyone must obey the law, but everyone is free to worship as they choose.

We are a nation that guarantees religious freedom.

Terror is meant to frighten people. It cannot defeat us."

The President Declares War on Terror

"We have been fighting the War on Terror since the attack on the Twin Towers.

Our military includes the Army, the Navy, the Air Force, the Marines, and the Coast Guard, as well as the Reserve Armed Forces.

The Army's elite force is called Special Operations. The Navy's elite force is the SEALs.

Our Intelligence agencies spent years planning a way to capture and punish the evil man who ordered the attack on the Twin Towers, Usama bin Laden.

On May 1, 2011, Usama bin Laden was located in Pakistan, captured, executed, and buried at sea according to the practices of his religion. It was almost ten years after his attack on us.

All the military worked together to capture Usama bin Laden. Navy SEAL Team 6 went into his house and seized him. Army Special Operations played a crucial role.

The Soldier speaking to you today was part of the Army Team that helped."

Silence filled the classroom.

SGT Bear stood quietly, respecting the silent reaction.

It was a lot for anyone to understand.

Until today, no one in his family ever knew that SGT Bear was part of the team that ended the life of the man who killed many innocent Americans.

"Students, you have been very respectful. You have listened carefully. Thank you for the way you have treated me. Do you have any questions?"

Little Bear's Class Asks Questions

A small hand shot up quickly. It was Tommy's hand. He was sitting in the front row. His attention to the speaker was rapt. He could hardly wait to ask.

"SGT Bear, Sir, did you kill anybody?"

SGT Bear dreaded this question.

SGT Bear thought, "What will Little Bear think of me if I say yes?

What will Ms. Green think of me if I say yes?

What will my wife, Lady Bear, think of me if I say yes?"

SGT Bear knew Tommy because Little Bear and Tommy often played together after school.

"Tommy, thank you for asking your question. Most everyone has the same question in mind, but only a child is honest enough to ask it."

Combat Action Badge

SGT Bear pointed to a silver medal with an oak leaf wreath on the left side of his dress blue blouse.

"Tommy, this is the Combat Action Badge. It has a symbol of a bayonet and a grenade, weapons of war. The oak leaf wreath is a symbol of strength and loyalty.

Soldiers who have been in close contact with the enemy earn the Combat Action Badge."

The class, attentive, was observing everything SGT Bear did and said.

"Sometimes, the enemy must be killed.

Soldiers do not want to kill anyone.

The enemy often attacked us in the dark of night. We have unique eyewear that helps us see at night, but it is far unlike seeing in the brightness of daylight.

"Tommy, the truthful answer to your question is this. I don't know if I killed anyone. I believe this is true for most Soldiers.

We have to stop the enemy from killing us. We have to halt the enemy in their country before they can come here and harm us."

War is Gruesome

"War is horrible, Tommy. It is one of the worst things in the world.

The only thing worse than war is losing a war.

America has never lost a war.

America keeps a powerful Army.

Sometimes, we have to show our strength to prevent a war.

Sometimes, we have to fight a small war before it becomes a big war.

We do not want war. We want peace.

To get peace, we have to have an active Army to protect the peace. America tries to get nations to live in peace with each other.

Tommy, Ms. Green, Little Bear, and all the children in Ms. Green's class do not have to worry about war.

Soldiers are here to protect you.

Soldiers are here to protect everyone in our beautiful and wonderful nation."

Ms. Green Speaks

"SGT Bear," said Ms. Green, "tell us about the education and training Soldiers must have."

Ms. Green did not want her class to get bogged down in thoughts of death that Soldiers have to accept.

Ms. Green wanted her class to be happy and feel

protected by our military forces.

Suddenly, Ms. Green stopped speaking. She stopped right in the middle of a sentence.

The students looked puzzled.

Ms. Green's Most Important Question

Right in the middle of thinking she wanted her students to be happy, she had an important question. She wanted her students to hear the answer to it.

Ms. Green is a sensitive teacher. She led up to her question slowly, carefully, and thoughtfully.

"First, before you tell us about your training, SGT Bear, let me thank you for what you do as a Soldier.

The Army protects us so we can raise our children in the freedom that you and our Soldiers fight every day to defend.

As you just said, these children can be free from the fear of enemy attack.

You, and thousands of Soldiers like you, are willing to do whatever is necessary to keep us free.

Thank you, SGT Bear."

The class politely applauded.

Then Ms. Green asked her most important question for the sake of her students.

No one in the class will ever forget Ms. Green's question and SGT Bear's answer.

"Let me rephrase Tommy's question, SGT Bear.

Would you be willing to be killed fighting for this country?"

SGT Bear's Reply

The class became quiet and still. All eyes focused on SGT Bear.

"Yes, mam," he answered. I made up my mind the day I joined the Army. I am willing to give my life to save our country if it is necessary."

Of course, I want to live. I want to raise my son. I want to be a good father. I want to be a good husband.

If the time comes, I will not hesitate to give my life for my fellow Soldiers.

Soldiers care for each other in combat. We are firmly attached to each other in the fighting.

I know that the Soldier on my left and the Soldier on my right will also give their life to save mine if it is ever necessary."

The sincerity of SGT Bear's reply was touching. The

absolute and seemingly endless silence that filled Ms. Green's classroom that day remains unsurpassed. Her students had never been more attentive or more grateful to her or any other guest speaker.

Little Bear's eyes filled with tears, but they were tears of pride. He never knew how much his dad loved his country and his fellow Soldiers.

After another very long pause, SGT Bear talked about training young men and women to be Soldiers.

Little Bears' classmates respected the tears they saw in the eyes of SGT Bear.

He talked about training Soldiers to be warriors.

He talked about combat deployments, and being sent far away to fight for our country.

He did not want it, but that day SGT Bear became the class hero of Ms. Green's sixth-grade class. The class committed itself to do some great things for their newly honored hero. No one could imagine the amazing things that would happen in only a few days.

6

SOMETHING VERY IMPORTANT

When Tommy came to school the next day, he was excited. His eyes widened. He could not sit still. He spoke rapidly, so fast it was easy to mistake what he said.

"Tommy," said Ms. Green, his kind, and usually very patient teacher, "you are disturbing our class' Quiet Time. Take down your hand, please."

"But Ms. Green, I have to tell you now."

"You know the rules, Tommy. We are no longer permitted to say the Lord's Prayer or pledge our allegiance to the American flag. In its place, we are only allowed to have a Quiet Time at the beginning of each school day.

You must respect the rights of your classmates to pray or meditate silently during Quiet Time. You may not ask questions, Tommy."

"This is not a question, Ms. Green. I just want to tell you something you need to know now." He was so eager that he was stomping his feet loudly.

"It must wait."

We will never know just how Tommy contained himself for the next 10 minutes, but somehow he sat quietly at his desk. He may have even prayed. He closed his eyes for 5 five minutes.

"Class," said Ms. Green, "take out your science texts, and open them to the third chapter.

Now you may come to my desk, Tommy, if you still must tell me something."

Serious News

"Ms. Green," said Tommy, "Little Bear's father is going back to the war."

Ms. Green looked very surprised. It was the second week of the new school year for her sixth-grade class. SGT Bear had spoken to the class only last week. He had not mentioned that he was soon to leave his family again. He did not say he was ordered to deploy.

It was serious news that SGT Bear was leaving for combat immediately. It was something critical for the Bear family as well as for the class.

Ms. Green shuddered. She felt chills up and down her back. Suddenly, she was fearful.

In her mind, Ms. Green could picture SGT Bear and his fellow Soldiers as they are boarding shiny steel jetliners. She could imagine the Soldiers landing, in just a few hours, in Iraq or Afghanistan. She felt the fear that all reasonable people feel going to a war zone.

Ms. Green's class had listened thoughtfully to SGT Bear as he explained the War on Terror. She knew her class would want to hear the news.

Ms. Green sensed a problem: what is the best way to tell her class that SGT Bear is returning to the War on Terror?

First, Ms. Green wanted to be confident that Tommy was correct.

She spoke calmly to Tommy. Students were still slowly taking out their science texts.

Ms. Green did not want her students to hear her conversation with Tommy. She motioned to him to come closer to her desk.

"Tommy," said Ms. Green in a serious tone, "how did you learn SGT Bear was leaving for the war? Did Little Bear tell you, Tommy?"

"Nobody told me, Ms. Green. I just listened," said Tommy.

"This is serious, Tommy. If no one told you SGT Bear was going back to war, how did you learn about it? "I just listened," you said."

"Little Bear's mother called my mom on the phone last night. I was doing my homework. When my mom started to cry, I listened carefully.

My mom said, "So, he's going to be gone a year? I know

you, Little Bear, and Chloe will miss him very much.

Try not to worry. We will do all we can to help." That's when my mother started crying."

Ms. Green talks to Little Bear and his Mother

"Class," said Ms. Green, "as you leave the building for recess, please do not run or speak in the hallway. Some classes are taking the SOLs today."

Ms. Green asked Little Bear to remain behind for a moment. Speaking softly, Ms. Green asked Little Bear if he were all right.

"Yes, Ms. Green. Why do you ask?"

"I understand that SGT Bear soon returns to combat."

"If he is," said Little Bear, "I haven't heard it."

Little Bear walked away. He did not want to miss recess.

Suddenly, Little Bear stopped. He returned to Ms. Green's desk.

With a grave look on his face, Little Bear said, "That may explain why my mother has been crying for the past few days."

He hesitated, appearing to be thinking deeply. Then he added, "Mother always cries before I know my dad is going to war.

She tries to be brave, but it does not work.

She loves him too much to be brave."

"I can understand that," said Ms. Green. "Does it also cause you to cry?"

"I try not to cry in front of people," said Little Bear, "but it upsets me when he leaves. I'm always afraid he will not come back."

"Are you scared that your dad will not survive combat?" asked Ms. Green.

Little Bear looked somber. "Yes, Ms. Green," said Little Bear; "we all heard what he said last week about dying for our country."

Ms. Green turned her head away. She did not want Little Bear to see the tears welling up in her eyes. She took a Kleenex to her eyeglasses, acting as if they were soiled.

"I won't keep you any longer, Little Bear. You may go to recess now."

That evening, Ms. Green phoned Little Bear's mother.

Yes, SGT Bear was going to Afghanistan on a special mission.

Yes, the notice was short, but not totally unexpected.

Yes, it was okay to tell Little Bear's classmates, but not to announce the destination. That's a military "secret," she said.

"It's not exactly a top secret. SGT Bear's unit just doesn't want many people to know exactly when and where they are going," said Little Bear's mother.

"They don't like for us to tell the clerks in the grocery stores. If we have a special meal, they do not want us to tell the people where we shop what is so unique that we are buying particular food or drinks."

Ms. Green understood that it was a matter of security.

"We would like to give SGT Bear a Going Away party," said Ms. Green.

"That would be okay," said Little Bear's mother. "You are very kind.

I know that would please my husband. He enjoyed speaking to your class. That's all he talked about for days.

He kept saying that you and your class were so intelligent. He told me you made him feel understood. "Ms. Green's class caused me to feel so proud to be a Soldier," he said.

Thanks."

Something for SGT Bear

In the next day, Ms. Green to her students, "Class, how many of you remember SGT Bear's visit and his talk last week?"

The entire class raised its hands.

"How many recall what SGT Bear told us?"

Again, all the class raised its hands.

"Who can tell me what he said?

Good.

When I call on you by name, tell me one thing he said.
Don't repeat what another student said before your turn.

Do you understand, class?

Good.

All right. Tommy, you are first."

"A Soldier is willing to die for his country."

"Yes."

"James, you are next."

"War is ugly."

"Mary."

"The only thing worse than war is losing a war."

"Josh."

"We don't have to worry because Soldiers protect us."

"Excellent, Josh.

Little Bear, tell us what impressed you the most."

"My dad helped capture Usama bin Laden, the man who ordered the attack on the Twin Towers. I didn't know that until he told us in his talk."

"Yes, Little Bear. He honored us with his secret. Your dad is very brave. He is also very humble. He did not want to boast. I believe he told us about his role in the capture of Usama bin Laden because he wanted you, Little Bear, to be proud of him.

"Kimberly."

"He gave us Krispy Kreme doughnuts. I enjoyed them very much."

"You said the magic phrase, Kimberly, 'he gave us...'

Yes, he gave us our tasty treat, and he gave us a talk that I will never forget.

How many students think we must give something to SGT Bear?"

Once again, the entire class raised its hands.

"SGT Bear is going back to combat. It is not his first trip. He has to leave earlier than he thought. Let's give him a 'going away' party."

The class cheered so loudly that the assistant principal came to see if the class was out of control.

When he heard the plan to show appreciation for SGT Bear, he cheered so loudly that the principal came to Ms. Green's class.

Guess what?

The principal not only cheered, but he exercised his right to whistle. The principal was known to have the loudest whistle in Prince George County, Virginia.

The children covered their ears with their hands to help block out the shrill sound of the principal's whistle.

It didn't work. Some people said that they heard the whistle noise a mile away.

That was the final stamp of approval.

Yes, all agreed. There would be a party for SGT Bear. One he would not forget.

Planning the Party for SGT Bear

"We will plan the party together," said Ms. Green.

"I will provide the refreshments. What does the class think SGT Bear would like?"

The class settled the refreshment decision. The students will serve Krispy Kreme Doughnuts with hot tea or a cold drink. Everyone agreed on the refreshments.

A problem came up, however, over a class gift for SGT Bear.

The Class Gift for SGT Bear

Some students wanted to give SGT Bear presents from their homes. Some wanted to bring money from home. Others suggested a big Teddy Bear.

Their feelings were strong. They wanted to show SGT Bear how much they cared.

Some of the boys received an in-class suspension for pushing each other down on the playground. They were fighting over "the best gift for SGT Bear."

Several girls cried when the boys laughed at their suggestions for "the best gift for SGT Bear."

Ms. Green got no help from the assistant principal or the principal for their recommendations regarding the class gift.

The Best Idea

It took no time to get the best idea for SGT Bear's gift, but it took several hours to get the question to the right person.

Tommy had served two hours of in-class suspension for fighting. He raised his hand to ask a question.

Ms. Green ignored him.

With his hand high in the air, Tommy loudly cleared his throat.

Ms. Green ignored him.

Now his hand was waving wildly in the air while he stomped his feet on the wooden classroom floor.

Ms. Green, annoyed, turned her head quickly to the ruckus. "Tommy, can you not ask a question calmly?" she asked.

"Yes, Ms. Green. Sorry. Why don't we ask Little Bear?" he said.

"Ask Little Bear what, Tommy?"

"The best gift for his dad," said Tommy.

Ms. Green knew Tommy was exactly right.

She should have thought of it herself.

She apologized to Tommy for responding, as she said, "rudely to rudeness."

"I forgive you, Ms. Green. But please don't let it happen again."

The class roared with laughter.

Tommy felt sheepish. Was it his turn to apologize again?

The spirit of forgiveness filled the classroom.

Students smiled as they turned their attention to their work.

Ms. Green made no comment. She smiled inside, but it did not show on her face.

Time for Action

When the period of Quiet Time for Individual Study ended, Ms. Green asked her class to listen to a progress report on SGT Bear's party.

At this particular time, nothing was more important to this teacher and her students alike than SGT Bear's party.

"Class, the party is an important project. What does a successful project require," she asked?

The class had not thought of the party as a project. The students just wanted to have fun and wish SGT Bear well.

No one spoke.

"A successful project requires planning.

We have planned the refreshments. I will provide those. Tommy's mother is going to help me with that.

It requires a time and place. We need to ask SGT Bear what time suits him best."

Little Bear raised his hand.

"What is it, Little Bear?" Ms. Green seemed impatient.

"Today is Tuesday," said Little Bear. "My dad leaves Thursday. The party will have to be tomorrow."

Ms. Green had no idea that no time remained for planning the party.

"Oh, my," said Ms. Green.

She was extremely surprised. She was quite shocked. Her feelings were evident from the expression on her face. It looked as if Ms. Green was frightened.

"I had no idea," said Ms. Green. "I need more time. I wanted us to plan this well.

Now we must act.

What in the world will we do for a gift?"

Ms. Green felt like a balloon that was stuck with a pin. The entire balloon's air had rushed out.

Ms. Green appeared sad. She slowly walked back to her desk.

She wrung her hands.

She looked around the room. She was searching for an answer.

All the students felt sad, too. All but one student felt bad.

Little Bear smiled and raised his hand.

Ms. Green nodded that it was okay for Little Bear to speak.

"I know what my dad wants more than anything."

Ms. Green's mood suddenly lifted.

"Tell us, Little Bear. Tell us what SGT Bear wants."

"I know because I heard him tell my mother how much he liked our class.

My dad wants a good quality photograph of our class.

He intends to take the photo himself, so it will always be on his cell phone.

A second thing he would like is a letter from the class every month he is gone.

He wants to know how we are doing and what we are doing while he is away.

Mail Call is the most important part of the day for Soldiers. To receive a letter from home is a joy to a Soldier in combat. Every day, Soldiers look for letters from home. Many never receive a letter from home. These "mail watchers" never know the joy of a letter from home, but they keep expecting it.

Do you think, Ms. Green, that my dad could take a picture of the class during the party tomorrow?

Do you believe the class could also send him a letter every month?"

Ms. Green's balloon was suddenly filled now with pure happiness. It could nearly burst.

"Little Bear, the camera may break if I'm in it!"

The class laughed because Ms. Green was so kind she was beautiful.

"Class, can we give SGT Bear what he asks of us?"

The class started clapping, whistling, stomping feet, and howling so that the assistant principal came down again and joined in.

The school principal started whistling even before he entered the room.

If happiness could be grabbed and placed on scales to weigh, Ms. Green's class would have broken the scales.

Ms. Green asked the class if the school principal and assistant principal could also be in the picture.

If SGT Bear wanted the administrator's' picture, it could be a separate shot, a decision based on a secret ballot.

The class revisited its decision later for reasons to be explained.

7

MAKING A SAD DAY HAPPIER

Late Tuesday night, Little Bear woke up suddenly from a fitful, restless sleep. Startled and afraid, he could feel his heart pounding.

Little Bear knew something was wrong, but he could not say what it was.

"Why do I feel like I've been running a long race," Little Bear thought. "I know I am in my bed. I know I've been asleep. I know it's still dark outside.

What's wrong with me?"

Little Bear had a queasy feeling in his stomach. He felt like he might get sick.

His throat was so dry it was painful to speak.

Little drops of sweat formed on his forehead. He could feel the little hairs on the back of his neck beginning to stand up. He felt as if he had a chill.

He was fully awake. Was it time to get up and dress for school?

No matter how hard he tried, Little Bear could not go back to sleep. What is worse, Little Bear's heart was still pounding.

He got out of bed, slid on his Army slippers, and walked slowly to his parents' bedroom.

He did not want to wake his dad. It was a "house rule" never to wake his dad suddenly.

Since the first day his father returned from combat, he could not stand being awakened by a loud noise or by any unexpected cause. In fact, he liked no surprises of any kind. He wanted no changes. Safety was always on his mind.

Little Bear will never forget how horribly upset his dad became when someone abruptly awakened him.

Tiptoeing, Little Bear quietly stood beside his mother's side of the bed.

Amazing to Little Bear, his mother was completely awake.

She motioned to Little Bear with one finger to her lips, telling him not to speak.

His mother took Little Bear's hand into hers, and they silently crept back to Little Bear's room.

"I'm not surprised you are awake, Little Bear," said Lady Bear. "I never sleep the night or two before your Dad goes back to war.

Let's talk about the sad day we are soon facing, the day he leaves.

We have to make a sad day into a happier one. We must do that for your dad."

What was Wrong with Little Bear?

Little Bear's mother was wide awake, but she was calm. She always understood.

"Why did you come to my room, Little Bear?" she asked.

"I don't know," said Little Bear. "I woke up with a start, frightened, and with a pounding heart.

I was afraid at first, but now I feel better that you are here."

"Did you have a bad dream?" asked his mother.

"I didn't think of that until you asked. Now, I remember having a nightmare. All I can remember about the dream was my dad. Yes, it was something bad about dad. I don't want to think about the dream now."

"What was your feeling in the dream, Little Bear? The dreamer's feelings might be the most important part of a dream."

Immediately, Little Bear said, "Oh, I remember my feelings in the dream all right. I was frightened and very gloomy," said Little Bear.

Tears slowly filled Lady Bear's eyes. The silent tears soon made streams down her cheeks. The darkness before dawn hid her tears from Little Bear, but he could hear his mother quietly begin to cry.

"I don't want to upset you, mother," said Little Bear. "I'll be alright."

"You are not upsetting me, Little Bear. What I'm feeling now is "sweet sorrow" because your dream tells me how much you love your dad. It tells me how much you also miss him when he goes back to war."

Little Bear Makes his Mother Proud

"It makes me so proud of you to share your dad with your classmates. Your father is becoming the "Class Dad" for your class.

The class party for your dad is only a few hours away.

Little Bear, you invited him to speak to your class, and now you are sharing your father with your whole class.

Do you know how wonderful that is?"

Little Bear did not know how to answer his mother. He wanted to be honest, but he also did not want to disappoint her.

Little Bear and his mother sat on the side of his bed in silence.

She wanted an answer.

Little Bear's mother repeated the question.

Little Bear answered her question with a question.

"Is it normal to have more than one feeling about the same thing, Mother?"

"Yes, it's okay to have more than one feeling about the same thing, because we can have more than one thought about the same thing, Little Bear."

"Will you please explain what you just said, Mother? I don't understand."

Little Bear's Mother Explains Thoughts and Feelings

"Too often we confuse 'feelings' and 'thoughts.'

I asked if you knew something. I asked if you knew how wonderful it is for you to share your dad with your classmates.

You answered by asking if it is okay to have more than one feeling about the same thing.

Little Bear, learn this lesson now, and you will make wise decisions: *our feelings come from our thoughts.*

There is a good way to know that what I said is true. You can conduct an experiment of your own to see if your feelings always come from thoughts.

The next time you have a strong feeling, stop and ask

yourself one question: what went through my mind just before I had that feeling.

Can you now understand why it is important to be certain that what you think is true?"

"Yes, I think I know why we need to think correctly. If we believe that something is true when it is false, we can feel bad for the wrong reason. When we know the truth, we can be free of thoughts that cause us to feel bad for no good reason."

Little Bear Tells his Mother the Truth

"I want you to be proud of me, mom. I think it's okay that Ms. Green gives dad a party.

I believe it's okay that dad speaks to my class.

I believe it's great that I have a Soldier for my dad.

I like it that my class likes dad, but I don't like sharing my dad with my classmates.

Now, I've said it.

Now you may think I'm stingy.

Now you may not be proud of me that much. I'm sorry."

The sun was gently bringing some daylight into Little Bear's bedroom.

He could see his mother smiling.

She hugged him tightly, and said, "I love you so much, Little Bear."

He could not have been more surprised.

"I thought you would hate me for being selfish and stingy."

"Little Bear, I love you for many reasons. I love your honesty.

I know you, my son. You are not selfish, and you are not stingy."

Little Bear learns Something New about his Classmates and his Teacher

"Little Bear," said his mother, "I want to tell you something you don't know about your teacher, and about your classmates.

I am not asking you to feel sorry for them. They would not want that.

I am telling you because I want you to understand them. I refer to this as the truth that will help set you free from unwanted or mistaken thoughts."

Little Bear became Informed

Little Bear was wide awake now.

No longer afraid or upset, Little Bear listened carefully to his mother.

"Ms. Green's father died when she was a little girl. Her mother reared her.

Have you ever met Tommy's father?"

"No, mother; I've never met Tommy's dad."

"You have never met Tommy's father because he has not taken part in Tommy's life. He left Tommy and his mother when Tommy was very young.

How many boys and girls in your class are reared by their mother alone, or with the help of grandparents?"

"I don't know. I've seen some grandparents on Grandparents Day at our school," said Little Bear.

Little Bear's mother stood up. Looking sad, she said, "Half of your classmates have no father.

Can you see how wonderful it is for them to know and respect your dad?"

Little Bear thought how bad it must be to have no father. His thought made him feel down.

Little Bear said, "My classmates seem to be doing okay without a dad. I can't tell who has no dad."

"That's because their mothers are doing a good job. Their

friends help. Their churches help. Their teachers help."

People who Give by Sharing

"Tommy never told me about his dad," Little Bear said. "I wondered why?"

Little Bear's mother suggested that Tommy might be ashamed of him.

Little Bear pondered her comments over and over in his mind. Then he said, "Mother, let's invite Tommy's mom and his sister, Chloe, to dad's farewell party at school."

"Little Bear, that's a magnificent idea. Shall I call Tommy's mother?"

"No, I want to invite them. I'll call them before I leave for school today."

It was beautiful to see Mother and son communicating this way.

Little Bear makes a Phone Call

Chloe answered the phone. "Hello, this is the Three Bears' residence; who is calling, please?"

"Chloe, this is Little Bear. May I speak to your mother?"

"She cannot come to the phone, Little Bear. Give me your message for her. I'll see that she gets it."

"I want you and your mother to come to my dad's farewell party in Ms. Green's classroom."

"I accept your invitation on behalf of my mom and myself. We'd love to be there. Tommy is excited. It's all he talks about."

"One more thing, Chloe, what's all this nonsense about, "Hello, this is the Three Bears' residence?""

"It's not nonsense, smartie. I believe it is the home of the Three Bears. If you have a problem with it, I am sorry. Someday, I'll set you straight."

"Chloe, I apologize. I did not mean to upset you. I just find it interesting.

See you at the party. Goodbye."

Ms. Green's Dad

Little Bear thought about what his mother was saying.

"What happened to Ms. Green's dad?" he asked.

His mother hesitated, and then she said, "I was afraid you would ask me that question.

He was a Soldier killed in action in a war against communism. It was called the Vietnam War. It started many years ago."

90

Getting Ready for School

Little Bear had not slept much the night before, but he was energetic and eager to get dressed for school. It was a special day. It was the day of his dad's farewell party.

Before leaving for his short walk to school, he asked two important questions: at what time the party starts, and at what time his dad leaves tomorrow?

The school party starts at 10 AM today, and Little Bear's father leaves from the Field House on Post, also at 10 AM tomorrow.

Little Bear left for school, stopped on the porch, came right back into the house, and asked his mother if she were coming to the party at school.

"No, Little Bear, parents were not invited."

Hearing that parents were left out, upset Little Bear.

"I want you to come to my class party. We are honoring dad, but I think we also need to honor you, too. You are a very important person. Will you attend?"

"Yes, Little Bear, I will participate in the class party. No one could turn down an invitation like yours. Thank you."

Little Bear's Special Feeling

As Little Bear walked to school that morning, he felt jubilant.

He remembered the experiment his mother mentioned several hours ago. "Ask yourself what went through your mind just before you had a strong feeling."

Still thinking of applying the experiment, Little Bear talked out loud to himself. He didn't mind. No one was around. "Just before I felt happy, I thought how blessed I am to have a dad that my classmates like and respect. Yes, that was the thought I had, and yes, it was that thought that made me happy. There is evidence that my idea is correct.

I feel even more fortunate now. What thought made me feel even more comfortable? I will share my dad with my class. Yes, that thought made me jubilant."

Little Bear remembered his mother's way of describing a mixture of happiness and sadness. She called it "sweet sorrow."

"That's the way I feel toward Ms. Green now," Little Bear thought. "Yes, it is "sweet sorrow" because her father was a Soldier killed in the war."

Little Bear was almost at the school house door when he decided he liked the experiment and was going to try to remember to use it to help understand his thoughts and his feelings, and how they are connected.

"Good morning, everybody," Little Bear said as he entered his class.

Ms. Green smiled.

His classmates were surprised because Little Bear had not ever been that friendly or happy before.

The Party

SGT and Mrs. Bear arrived exactly and precisely on time. The class stood out of respect for SGT Bear.

"You may take your seats, Class," announced Ms. Green.

"SGT and Mrs. Bear," said Ms. Green, "I have placed two chairs for you in front of the class. Please make yourselves comfortable.

Please feel warmly welcomed by my class and me, and by the school administration.

Your presence here today honors us, SGT Bear because you represent the Soldiers who fight for our freedom.

These children are learning that freedom is not free.

They are learning that our Soldiers help pay the cost of our liberty. These students are learning that our Soldiers help keep us free.

SGT Bear, you spoke to us last week. We remember everything you said, but we would like to give you the opportunity to talk once again today."

SGT Bear Speaks

Ms. Green's sixth-grade class was quiet and respectful.

SGT Bear stood at attention. He appeared stern and commanding. "Ms. Green, School Administration, and students, I have never had a party given in my honor before today. I thank you. My wife thanks you. And my son, Little Bear, wants to thank you. The memory of you and your party for me will be dear. I will keep it in my heart and my mind forever. Let the party begin."

8

FAREWELL PARTY

No party ever began on a more excited note.

The children applauded loudly when SGT Bear said, "Let the party begin."

Whistling and dancing, with tightly held hands, they formed a ring around their guests. SGT Bear pulled Little Bear into the circle. Lady Bear pulled Ms. Green into the circle.

The class roared happily. Holding hands tighter than ever, they continued to dance and sing as they went around and around their honorees.

And who do you think came in next?

You guessed it. First, the assistant principal, and then the principal rushed into Ms. Green's classroom.

I can't explain how it happened because it happened so fast, but at first, the assistant principal, and then the principal ended up in the center of the circle.

Soon a chant evolved. At first, it was not easy to make out what the students were chanting. The words of the song were not clear. Everyone was yelling and nearly out of breath.

It turned out the students were singing and shouting, "For he's a jolly good fellow...and so say all of us."

"Is There a Riot in There?"

Three members of the SWAT Team knocked loudly on Ms. Green's door.

They shouted, "Are you all right in there?"

Ms. Green tried to reply, but she had no strength remaining in her voice. She could barely speak above a whisper.

 The SWAT Team shouted, "We are coming in at the count of 3. When we get in, hit the floor," they commanded.

"No, no," shouted the principal. "We are having a party. Come and join us."

The SWAT Team replied, "We got a 911 phone call, saying there was a riot in this school. Was that a prank call?"

"I believe it was a misunderstanding, Officer. We are having a Farewell Party for a Soldier returning to combat."

"Since that's the case," said the SWAT Team spokesman, still outside Ms. Green's closed door, "we will be happy to join you. We were all Soldiers several years ago. Are we still invited?"

The principal opened the door and greeted the SWAT Team.

The SWAT Team took off their helmets and their outer jackets after they saluted SGT Bear.

Finally, the honorees were all released from their circle. Everyone was still smiling, and everyone was tired.

The Lunch Room Staff

The lunch room staff brought in the refreshments. The lunch room staff was also in a good mood.

"Class, and honored guests, including our surprise guests, we never had a party like this one, but I think it was the best party I ever attended," said Ms. Green.

"Does the administration wish to speak?"

"Not a word," said the principal, "except to say God Bless SGT Bear and his family."

Everyone cheered loudly.

"And God Bless you, Ms. Green, and your entire class."

Louder cheering and whistling.

"When I retire next spring, Ms. Green, I want you and your class to be in charge of my retirement party."

Even more and even louder and even longer cheering burst out. The party finally settled down, but not until it ate all the refreshments.

The "Class Picture"

Ms. Green raised both her arms high into the air, signaling her class to settle down, be quiet, and listen.

Surprisingly, the class instantly became as quiet as church mice.

"SGT Bear, this party is for you. We understand the only gifts you want from us are a class photo, to be taken by you on your cell phone, and a letter from the class every month you are away.

Is that correct, SGT Bear?"

"Yes, Ms. Green," said SGT Bear, "that is correct.

May I speak to your class and you, Ms. Green?"

"Of course."

"I will always smile when I remember this party.

Thank you, Ms. Green.

Thank you, Class.

Thank you, Assistant Principal.

Thank you, Principal.

Thank you, lunch room staff.

Thank you, SWAT Team.

I want everyone here to pose for the "Class Picture."

SGT Bear had the newest cell phone available. It could take a panoramic photo.

Everyone moved in as close as possible.

SGT Bear took the "Class Picture." It turned out well.

He took many other pictures of the class, the teacher, the administration, the lunch room staff, and the SWAT Team.

"Thank you, everyone," said SGT Bear. "You will always be in my thoughts. Thank you."

The Special Announcement

"SGT Bear's unit will leave tomorrow at 10 AM from the Post Field House," announced the Principal.

"If you wish to attend the ceremony tomorrow, you must bring a note from home. A parent must give his or her consent for you to participate.

I'm making a school bus available for the trip.

I intend to be there myself," said the principal.

"May we attend?" asked the lunch staff.

"May we attend?" asked the SWAT Team.

"All who wish to show their appreciation and respect for our Soldiers may attend," the principal firmly stated. Everyone applauded. Thankfully, the shouting had ended, at least for now.

Chloe's Invitation

Chloe raced directly to SGT Bear.

"May I speak with you, SGT Bear? My name is Chloe. Tommy is my brother."

Surprised, SGT Bear, not knowing Chloe, smiled and said, "Yes, Chloe, you may speak to me. What's on your mind?"

"Will you, Lady Bear, and Little Bear come to my church tonight?"

SGT Bear wanted to say no. He wanted to say that it was his last night in town. He wanted to say that he did not know her until now. He wanted to say her invitation came too late.

He cannot explain why, but SGT Bear looked into Chloe's eyes and said "Yes."

"It's our Wednesday Night Prayer Service. I want to pray for your safety. I want to pray that God will protect you and bring you home safely to your family." In a soft whisper, making it necessary for SGT Bear to bend his head closer to Chloe to hear her, Chloe added, "And I want God to bring my father home safely to me.

I also want to pray for your family. Will you bring Lady Bear and Little Bear with you?"

SGT Bear did not hesitate. He had a sudden feeling of peace. "We will come as a family to your Wednesday Night Prayer Service tonight, Chloe. Thanks for your invitation."

A Child's Faith

Chloe's small church, seating not more than 25 people, was located in Hopewell, Virginia, near Fort Lee. Chloe, Tommy, and their mother, Betty, sat quietly on the front row.

A woman softly played the piano. Chloe hummed the words to the familiar Baptist hymn, "What a Friend we have in Jesus."

In a rusty, folding, gray metal chair, Rev. Earle Doyle Beale sat on the stage facing the audience. His round, friendly face radiated kindness. His eyeglasses, rimmed with silver, were thick. His red wavy hair was receding, making him appear slightly bald.

Rev. Beale wore a white shirt without a necktie and a navy blue blazer. He held a thin, worn, black Bible in his hands.

Occasionally, looking up from the Bible, his closed eyes suggested he was praying.

Chloe said, "Mother, may I please go to the church door to greet the Bears?"

With her mother's consent, Chloe quietly, but quickly walked to the church door,   getting there the very moment the Bears walked in.

Chloe said, "Hello, Lady Bear, SGT Bear, and Little Bear." Chloe behaved like a deaconess. With her outstretched hand, she warmly greeted each Bear, individually.

"I'm so happy to see you. I *knew* you would keep your promise.

Please follow me."

Chloe and her family, and the Bear family filled the front row of the little church.

Rev. Beale began the prayer service with this opening prayer:

"Dear Father in Heaven, your Son, Jesus, promised that where two or three gather in His name, He will be present. We sincerely pray a prayer of thanksgiving for that unbroken promise.

Come into our hearts now, Lord Jesus. Come into our prayer service. We are gathered here in Hopewell in Your

Name. Send to us now the Comforter, the Spirit of Truth, the Teacher, the Holy Spirit to walk beside us. Forgive us for the sins that darken our pathway to you.

Shine Your light of hope on every person here tonight, and grant us peace. Hear us, Dear Lord, as we trust you to meet every need. We pray in the name of the Father, the Son, and the Holy Spirit. Amen.

"If you have a prayer request," Rev. Beale said to the small congregation, "please stand now and make your request."

The pianist softly played Amazing Grace.

A few minutes of silence ended when Chloe stood up.

Rev. Beale motioned to the pianist. The music stopped.

Rev. Beale said, "Chloe, do you have a prayer request?"

"Yes, Sir."

"What is your prayer request, Chloe?"

"SGT Bear is sitting on the front row tonight because I asked him to come to my church so we can pray for him.

He is going to Afghanistan tomorrow morning to fight for our freedom. I want God to protect him. I want God to take care of his family while he is away. I want God to bring him back just as he is tonight, or even better.

I don't want SGT Bear to come back from the War on

Terror like my dad did. The war changed him so much that he got angry all the time, and then he finally left us.

I also want God to bring my dad back to us as he was before the war.

I hope my prayer request is not too long, Rev. Beale.

Sometimes, my mother says I pray too long. I'm sorry, but I just had to tell Jesus what's on my mind. I know He listens. I know He wants to answer our prayers."

There were no dry eyes on the front row.

Rev. Beale removed his eyeglasses. He unfolded a large white handkerchief, and he tried to dry his eyes.

"Halleluiah, Halleluiah. Praise God." Rev. Beale's face and voice shone as if glowing with the bright light of joy.

"Thank you, Chloe, for showing us what God wants us to be. Your faith and trust in our Lord is a beautiful example for us to follow."

Sincerely touched by Chloe's prayer request, Rev. Beale kept thanking God.

Then, Rev. Beale asked SGT Bear to come forward and kneel. Chloe went with him to the front of the church, holding SGT Bear's right hand.

"I'm going to ask SGT Bear's wife and son to come forward and stand next to him.

Tommy, you and Betty, please come up as well.

I'm going to ask each one of you to lay a hand on SGT Bear as I pray for him."

The congregation was caught up in the Spirit of Truth. Some people formed a ring around SGT Bear. Other people knelt in prayer at their seats, and some stood and prayed.

Prayer for SGT Bear

"Dear Heavenly Father, we bring the requests of this child to you, with humble, obedient hearts and thankful minds. Attend this child, we pray and grant her the blessings of her prayers according to your will. The words of her prayers go up to you with the thoughts of all of us who are gathered here tonight in one accord in your name.

Chloe is asking you to protect SGT Bear, a Soldier willing to lay down his life for his friends, for his country.

You have commanded us to love one another. Help us to keep all your commandments. In particular, help us to love one another.

You have said, "Greater love has no one than this, that one lay down his life for his friends." SGT Bear is willing to show the greater love, Lord, but we entreat you to surround him with your angels when he is in danger.

Chloe is asking you to protect SGT Bear's family in his

105

absence. Guide us, Lord, to be under the power of your will in this and all the requests made here tonight.

Lord, we don't know Chloe's father, but we hear her passionate plea for his safety, wellbeing, and return to his family. You know the strength of a father's love for his children. Let that love lead Chloe's father back home again, according to your will.

Chloe knows, Dear Lord, that war can injure the mind, but you made the mind of each human being. You are our Creator. Create in him, Dear Lord, a pure heart and a clean mind, O God. Restore to health the brokenness so Chloe's father can love again.

These heartfelt prayers come with sincerity and love. In the name of the Heavenly Father, His Son, Jesus Christ, and the Holy Spirit. Amen."

Ms. Green knew there was a Wednesday Night Prayer Meeting in Hopewell, but she did not attend. Ms. Green is a member of an Anglican Church. In her home where Ms. Green resides alone, she got on her knees in prayer for SGT Bear.

From the *Book of Common Prayer*, 1928, she prayed:

"Watch over thy child, O Lord, as his days increase; bless and guide him wherever he may be, keeping him unspotted from the world.

Strengthen him when he stands; comfort him when discouraged or sorrowful; raise him up if he falls; and in his heart may thy peace which passeth understanding abide all the days of his life; through Jesus Christ our Lord. Amen."

Ms. Green added: "Lord, I know that my prayer is ordinarily a prayer for a birthday. I think, in some important way, this is like a birthday for SGT Bear. He came into my life and to the life of my class as a new birth. He opened my eyes to the importance of all who serve in defense of our country. He is not without sin, O Lord, like Jesus was when He dwelt here on earth, but SGT Bear is willing to give his life for us.

As you can tell, O Lord, this prayer is from my heart for this brave Soldier and for all who are like him.

It is also a prayer for SGT Bear's family and the relatives of all who serve to keep us free. It is in the name of Our Savior, Jesus Christ our Lord that I pray. Amen."

9

TOMMY'S DISCOVERY

Tommy and Little Bear were walking home from school. It is something they did every school day. They usually talked and joked along the way home, but not today.

It was a cold, wet, late fall afternoon. The leaves were off the trees. Thick, gray clouds covered the sun, and the days were getting shorter, the daylight fading early.

Tommy was invigorated by the weather. "I hope it snows and snows tonight," he said.

Little Bear did not reply.

"I wouldn't care if it snowed so hard they closed the schools for a week. Wouldn't that be great, Little Bear?"

Tommy thought Little Bear must be daydreaming because his questions went unanswered. He did not press him for an answer.

"I bet I can jump higher than you, Little Bear. I 'm sure I can jump up and touch that Sycamore tree limb, straight ahead."

Like a flash of lightning, Tommy assumed the idealized role of NBA star, LeBron James, going up for a slam-dunk, but he barely missed the limb.

Excited, as usual, bragging as usual, and friendly as usual, Tommy shouted back to Little Bear, "Did you see how close I came to making that shot, Little Bear?"

Little Bear did not reply.

Tommy decided that something was wrong. Little Bear has perfect hearing. Tommy was confident he spoke loudly, but now he wondered what was wrong with his friend. Why would Little Bear not talk at all?

Why Little Bear did not Speak

Tommy knew there was one subject on which Little Bear could not be silent. Little Bear always talked about his dad, SGT Bear.

Tommy returned to Little Bear's side, joined him in a slower pace, and searched his mind for the best approach to discuss Little Bear's favorite person, his dad, SGT Bear.

The dialogue between Tommy and Little Bear went like this:

Tommy: "Little Bear, when is your dad coming home from the War on Terror?"

Little Bear: "I don't know." Little Bear spoke in a flat, lifeless, bored tone.

Tommy: "You don't sound interested. Do you care?"

Little Bear: "I care. I care too much."

Tommy: "Why do you say that? Why do you say you care too much?"

Little Bear: "I'm worried about my dad."

Tommy: "Why are you worried about him, Little Bear?"

Little Bear: "He stopped calling us."

Tommy: "What? I don't believe it."

Tommy was shocked. He was completely stunned.

Little Bear was sad.

Little Bear was fighting back the tears when he said: "We have not heard from him for the last two months. I don't know why."

Tommy was never at a loss for words, except now. He had no idea what to say. He did not want to make his friend more upset. He did not want Little Bear to think he was prying too deeply into his personal affairs.

After a long pause, Tommy said, "Did your parents fight?"

Little Bear: "I don't know."

Tommy: "Don't you care?"

Little Bear: "Maybe I care too much."

Tommy: "You keep saying, "Maybe I care too much." Is that your alibi?"

Little Bear: "I heard my mother crying in the middle of the night. I didn't get up.

She had been on the phone. It woke me up when she slammed down the phone."

Tommy: "When was that?"

Little Bear: "Two months ago. I think that's why he hasn't called back."

Tommy: "Is it another woman?"

Little Bear: "No, that's not it. It's related to money.

When my dad's deployed, my mother controls the money."

Tommy: "That's not fair. Can she spend the money however she pleases?"

Little Bear: "Yes, it's called the POA or Power of Attorney. It's an Army regulation."

Tommy: "I never heard of it. What is a Power of Attorney?"

Little Bear: "When a married Soldier gets deployed, he signs over the control of his finances to his wife. Some other responsible person gets the Power of Attorney If the Soldier is not married."

Tommy: "It does not seem fair. It is not fair!"

Little Bear: "It may not seem fair, but if the Soldier is far away in a war, there may be a crisis at home. Someone must be available to pay the bills for the Soldier. That's the way the Army sees it."

SGT Bear's Money

Tommy: "So what happened to SGT Bear's money?"

Little Bear: "My mother bought a new sports car. It was supposed to be a surprise for my dad. You know, sort of like a welcome home gift."

Tommy: "What happened?"

Little Bear: "One of my dad's buddies saw the car parked in our driveway. The word got back to my dad. I think someone asked my dad why he has a sports car parked in our driveway. That's when my dad stopped calling."

Tommy: "Why?"

Little Bear: "I don't know, but I think he wanted to save the money to buy a farm. Maybe that's why he stopped contacting us. I don't know why, but I believe he wanted to buy a hideaway. My dad wanted to get away from people. He wanted to feel safe; he said that before he left.

Mother likes the city, the bigger, and the better. She does not want to live far away on a farm or to get away from people.

My mother grew up on a farm. Many times, I've heard her say she wants to be a city girl now. She never intends to be a farm girl again."

Tommy: "Do you mind if I tell my mother about this? She's good with problems."

Little Bear: "I just want it to be like it was. He was so happy when he left."

Tommy: "Why was he so happy when he left? Did he want to leave home to get away from your mother?

Little Bear: "No, he's a Soldier. He wanted to help his unit. Also, the Farewell Party we gave him at school cheered up everybody."

Tommy: "It was a great party. There was one surprise after another."

Little Bear: "It's hard to understand, but most Soldiers want to go back to combat.

Soldiers think they have nothing to celebrate. The war is not over. They believe they have no victory.

Soldiers don't like leaving their families, but they want to finish the job over there.

My mother understands that feeling, and she supports my dad as a Soldier."

Tommy's Mother puts on her Thinking Cap

"Lady Bear, this is Betty, Tommy's mother. Do you remember me? I called you about the school party. It was the Farewell Party the class was giving for SGT Bear."

"Yes, Betty, I remember you very well. Tommy is Little Bear's best friend."

What Betty planned to do was not easy. She wanted to help, but she did not want her intentions misunderstood. Lady Bear might think she was emotionally trespassing, she feared.

Betty thought that Lady Bear might say, "Mind your own business," and hang up the phone.

"I'm calling to see how you are doing," Betty said.

"Things could be better, Betty. Things could be a lot better." Lady Bear sounded sad.

Betty thought it was the best time to start putting her plan into action.

Betty said, "I have some extra flowers I cut from my garden this morning. I wanted to bring them in the house before cold weather. May I bring them to you to help cheer up your day?"

Betty said a silent prayer, "Dear Lord, open Lady Bear's heart so that I may speak to her and restore hope where

115

there are such darkness and despair."

"I have not been receiving guests, Betty. My house is a mess. I haven't brushed my hair in days. I've been feeling like such a failure that I have not wanted to see anyone. More than that, I haven't wanted anyone to see me."

Betty repeated her silent prayer.

Then Betty said, "I know that feeling. I felt the same way when my husband left me."

Betty heard crying. That was all that she heard on the phone line. It seemed like it would never end, but Betty did not hang up.

After what seemed to be a long time, Lady Bear said, "Are you still on the line, Betty?"

"Yes."

"Thank you," said Lady Bear. "I would love some of your flowers."

Ms. Green Helps

Teachers can become attached to certain classes. Promotion was the case with Ms. Green and her sixth-grade class.

The school administration knew that Ms. Green's sixth-grade class had done well. Ms. Green was going to be promoted along with her class to the seventh grade next semester.

This exception to school policy turned out to be a real advantage for Little Bear, as these pages will reveal.

On the same day that Tommy's mother visited Lady Bear, Tommy did not go out to the playground for recess. This coincidence was unknown to him.

"Tommy," said Ms. Green, "are you ill?"

"No, Ms. Green," said Tommy. "I am not sick. I just feel kind of gloomy."

"I do not believe I've ever seen you this way," said Ms. Green. "You are always happy. You are usually doing things that make you and others happy.

You are always the first student on the playground at every recess."

Tommy explained to Ms. Green that he remained inside during recess to speak to her about Little Bear's problem.

"I'm too young to do much about it, Ms. Green, but I thought, I don't know, I just thought you could do something about it. I told my mother about it, too."

Ms. Green stopped everything she was doing and carefully listened to every word Tommy uttered. She was alarmed.

"I can't believe it, Tommy. As you know, our class writes a letter every month to SGT Bear.

He always replies the same day he receives our messages. His letters sound like he is doing fine. He even tries to cheer us up in his letters."

Ms. Green was shaking her head side to side in disbelief.

Tommy had tears in his eyes.

Tommy said, "But he has not contacted his family in 2 months. It's all based on a silly misunderstanding. What can we do, Ms. Green? SGT Bear is still our Class Hero."

Never more determined or more severe, Ms. Green answered Tommy.

"I don't know what we can do, Tommy, but we will not stop trying until this problem is solved. I give you my word, Tommy."

The Assistant Principal and the Principal Help

"Is it true that you were a Soldier before you became a teacher?" asked Ms. Green.

"Yes, that is true," said the Assistant Principal.

"Is it true that you served in Afghanistan and Iraq?"

"Yes, Ms. Green. Why do you ask me these questions now?"

Ms. Green explained her concerns for Little Bear, Lady Bear, and Tommy, his mother, and her class' relationship with SGT Bear.

"Is there any way you can help us?" she pleaded.

"This is a worthy cause for which you want help, Ms. Green, and I applaud you for it, but this is also a delicate matter."

"I don't understand," said Ms. Green. "How is it a delicate matter?"

"Because it may involve privileged communication," said the Assistant Principal. "What is said between a Soldier and his spouse is highly personal. A third party who hears about it has a duty to keep it confidential.

There are few exceptions to the rule, so to speak, but your worthy cause may be one of the exceptions."

"What can you do to help?"

"News gets around, Ms. Green," said the Assistant Principal. "I had already heard about this trouble before you came to see me today. That is why I was not surprised.

The school is already authorized to communicate with SGT Bear's unit. I will get the name of SGT Bear's Chaplain and contact him.

We will rely on the Chaplain to do what is best for all who are concerned."

There was no smile on Ms. Green's face when she left the Assistant Principal's Office, but there was a spirit of hope in her heart.

10

SGT BEAR'S CHAPLAIN

COL James Edward Walker found SGT Bear stationed in Kandahar, Afghanistan, only 5 miles from Headquarters, Chaplain Walker's duty office.

At this time of the year, it was cold and rainy in Kandahar.

"CPT Riley, you are SGT Bear's CO (commanding officer). What can you tell me about him, CPT?"

"SGT Bear is an outstanding Soldier. He is one of the best. Why do you ask, Chaplain, if I may ask?" said the CO.

"Of course you may ask, CPT Riley, but I may not be permitted to tell you everything. You understand. Let me just say there is some concern about SGT Bear expressed by his son and by his son's classmates at school."

"Now that you mention it, SGT Bear appears to have changed in the past couple of months."

"Changed?"

"Yes, all he wants to do is go on combat missions. The more dangerous the mission, the more likely he is to volunteer for the mission.

I had not paid much attention to it. SGT Bear does little else. Except for combat missions, he stays to himself, and he does not want to talk. He won't even go to "mail call."

I took his last letter to him. It was from Ms. Green's Class. I read that on the return address.

A few days later, I went back to his CHU (Container Housing Unit) and noticed he had not opened the letter.

It does not sound good, does it, Chaplain?"

The Chaplain did not reply. He was deep in thought.

"What did you say?" asked the Chaplain. "I just could not get the image of the unopened letter out of my mind."

CPT Riley repeated his question. "It does not sound right, does it?"

"How much longer is your deployment, CPT?"

"Our Advanced Party left for home two weeks ago. Unless we get extended, we will all be home in 30 days."

"Do you have a Behavioral Health Clinic nearby?" the Chaplain asked.

"Yes, Chaplain Walker, I'll get SGT Bear over there today."

SGT Bear sees a Psychiatrist

"SGT Bear," said the psychiatrist, "Welcome to Behavioral Health."

SGT Bear was very uncomfortable. He had never seen a

psychiatrist and did not want to see one now. His heart was pounding. Drops of sweat were forming on his forehead. He kept clearing his throat, and he was breathing fast.

SGT Bear was tense. He scanned the psychiatrist's office, searching for anything dangerous, anything from which he needed protection.

The psychiatrist waited patiently for a reply to his welcome. He had seen hundreds of tense combat Soldiers. Most had a "thousand mile stare," a unique gaze that looked sad, and is hard to define. SGT Bear had the same stare.

SGT Bear spotted a small photograph on the psychiatrist's desk. It had a thin gold frame. In bright color, the woman had golden hair. The two children, also blond with blue eyes, were dressed alike.

"Is that your family?" SGT Bear asked.

Pleased that SGT Bear would say anything, the psychiatrist smiled. "Yes, it's my wife and sons. Would you like to hold it and look at it closely?"

"No, sir," said SGT Bear. "I'm through with women. They can't be trusted. I'll never make that mistake again," SGT Bear growled, and he raised his voice.

"Can you tell me what happened to make you feel that

way, SGT Bear?"

"It would do no good. Words won't change the fact that my wife betrayed me."

SGT Bear looked away. He did not want to see the family photograph. His mind was made up. No psychiatrist was going to persuade him to change his mind.

"I'm here in your office today for one reason, and one reason alone. I'm here because my CO ordered me to come here for a Command Evaluation."

"SGT Bear, there may be other reasons you are here in my office today."

SGT Bear, more irritated now than earlier, shouted at the psychiatrist. "I demand that you tell me any other reason I'm here!

"Calm down, SGT Bear! Let's be reasonable. You have a right to know everything I know about your case."

SGT Bear was surprised. It caught him off guard.

First, he did not know he needed to calm down. Second, he wanted to know all the reasons his commander sent for a Command Evaluation. Third, he wanted to report anyone who knew about his private affairs without his consent.

SGT Bear gets a Psychiatric Diagnosis

"I will tell you now that many people care about you," said the psychiatrist. "I will say nothing else until I complete the psychiatric evaluation."

"What if I don't cooperate?" asked SGT Bear.

"Many people care about you, SGT Bear. Does that mean anything to you?"

SGT Bear did not reply, but somehow he was a little less irritated. His feeling of rage left, and he was less anxious. It made feel better to hear that others care for him.

"How many hours of sleep do you get?"

"I don't sleep."

"Why don't you sleep, SGT Bear?"

"Nightmares keep me from wanting to sleep. They make it too scary to fall asleep."

"What are your nightmares about?"

"Have you ever been on patrol?"

"We are not here to talk about me, SGT Bear.

How many years have served in the Army, SGT Bear?"

"Eight."

"How many combat deployments have you been ordered to take?"

"Five."

"How many months total have you had in combat, SGT Bear?"

"Sixty."

"SGT Bear," said the psychiatrist, "I believe you have PTSD."

SGT Bear knew the psychiatrist was correct, but he did not want to admit it.

What is Combat PTSD?

"I could tell you have PTSD," said the psychiatrist, "by the way you walked into my office. You were very cautious, jittery, hotheaded, and tense. In a flash, you scanned every corner of my office. You were on guard, and angry. You trusted no one. You flinched or jumped when I accidentally dropped my pen.

You suffer from nightmares. Your mood is depressed, so you enjoy nothing. You avoid people because you view them as dangerous. I could go on.

PTSD is nothing to be ashamed of, SGT Bear.

PTSD is a real injury to the mind. We can't see an injured mind like we can see an injured leg or arm or chest. The mind doesn't bleed. We can't bandage an injured mind.

A Soldier with PTSD has not lost his mind. PTSD does not
the person is "crazy."

PTSD does not affect intelligence.

In a word, PTSD sharpens a particular type of memory. A
Soldier with PTSD keenly recalls the worst parts of combat,
forgets little about the fighting, but almost entirely cannot
remember happy and pleasant memories.

PTSD is an injury to the mind that increases the brain's
ability to recall the horrible details of the trauma so that it
can prevent it from ever happening again.

Soldiers with PTSD become too cautious. They do not
want anything bad to happen to their loved ones, but
PTSD changes the way love is expressed. The ability to give
and receive love does not return until healing begins.

The injured mind of the Soldier with PTSD finds it difficult
to feel attached or close to others. The healing of PTSD
occurs when the Soldier learns that it is safe to become
attached again. The desire to get attached to others
returns very slowly, but it must be learned again.

To feel safe, Soldiers with PTSD want everything just right.
If things are not just right, they think that danger is lurking.
When things are not just right, "someone has not been
wise." If someone has not been wise, Soldiers with PTSD

become furious. It is always understood as dangerous when even tiny changes occur, no matter what they are, even when others cannot see the changes.

SGT Bear Learns the Truth

"To whom do you feel the closest, SGT Bear?" asked the psychiatrist.

"Do you mean now, or ever?"

"Both," said the psychiatrist.

"Before this deployment, I felt close to my wife and son. Now I only feel close to my son. I feel close to him because of his innocence. I know he loves me."

"Why have you lost your feelings for your wife, SGT Bear?"

"Have you ever been betrayed, Doc?"

The psychiatrist did not reply.

"My wife has my power of attorney. She can spend my money however and whenever she likes. She can also entertain anyone she wants.

Some dude has a sports car. The owner spends the night at my house. I know this because my friends care about me and they keep me informed.

Either my wife owns a new sports car, or someone living with her does."

SGT Bear was angrier now than at the beginning of the session. He was almost yelling. Breathing faster and speaking louder, SGT Bear was mad. His face was red and hot.

The psychiatrist, a patient and kind man by nature before becoming a psychiatrist, decided to let SGT Bear finish talking before he started to speak. He just sat quietly, but he was completely attentive.

"Is there a third possibility, SGT Bear?"

"What do you mean?"

SGT Bear was calmer and inquisitive.

The psychiatrist did not reply immediately.

"Doctor, I asked what you meant about a third possibility!"

"Could the sports car be a present for you?"

The SGT did not reply. He was baffled, confused, and even more doubtful.

"A present for me?"

"Yes," said the psychiatrist. "Could your wife have purchased the sports car for you? Could it be a welcome home gift for you, the only man she loves?"

"I never thought of that."

SGT Bear started to cry. He hated to cry. It made him feel weak, but he could not help himself. These were tears of shame. He blamed his wife for something she never did. Yes, he now painfully knew he had been completely wrong about Lady Bear. He covered his face with both hands, and he wept.

"How do you know that's what she did?" demanded SGT Bear.

"Do you know Chaplain Walker?" said the psychiatrist.

"Yes."

"Do you trust him?"

"So far, I have no reason not to believe him."

"May I ask him to join us?"

SGT Bear was surprised that the chaplain was nearby.

"Sure, bring him in."

An Explanation

Chaplain Walker explained the whole story to SGT Bear. It was a complicated story, but the chaplain made it clear.

"Little Bear told Tommy you had stopped calling or writing home.

Tommy told Ms. Green. She and her class care about you,

130

SGT Bear.

Ms. Green told the Assistant Principal.

The Assistant Principal had been a Soldier who served in the War on Terror.

He contacted the Unit Chaplain. That's me, SGT Bear.

I came to see you after I spoke to your CO, CPT Riley.

CPT Riley referred you to the psychiatrist."

The psychiatrist said, "That's me."

The chaplain continued. "In the meantime, Tommy's mother, Betty, called Lady Bear and met with her.

Lady Bear was very depressed. She felt she had lost you. Betty prayed with her and for her. Lady Bear does not know that Ms. Green was also working on a plan to help you, but she is feeling better.

SGT Bear, you are the hero of your son's school. No Soldier wants to be a hero, but that's who you are to Ms. Green's class.

They plan a Welcome Home Party for you that will be greater than your Farewell Party. From what I hear about the Farewell Party, that's going to be hard to beat."

SGT Bear's Future

Then the psychiatrist said something that surprised all those present.

"SGT Bear, your PTSD is severe. I want to offer you several weeks of treatment in our Army hospital at Landstuhl, Germany."

SGT Bear could not have been more shocked.

"Doc, please don't do that to me. Please, Doc, it will end my career.

We only have 30 days left in Afghanistan.

I want to come home on the airliner with my unit.

I want to step off the plane with my unit and be greeted by my family, like everyone else.

Please, doc. Please."

Chaplain Walker stood up. "I will take responsibility for SGT Bear," he said.

"I will see him daily while he is here.

You can treat him while he is here.

I will fly back with the unit.

I will make sure he goes to Behavioral Health at Fort Lee when he returns.

Doctor, I give you my word as a US Army Chaplain that SGT Bear will be all right."

Reluctantly, the psychiatrist agreed.

SGT Bear's Family greets Him

Chaplain Walker watched carefully as SGT Bear warmly hugged and kissed Lady Bear when his unit landed two weeks later at Langley Air Force Base in Virginia.

He also watched SGT Bear hug Little Bear, and whisper in his ear, "Thank you, Little Bear. I know what you did to help. Thank you."

Ms. Green was there. SGT Bear shook her hand vigorously, and he said, "Thank you, thank you, thank you. I will never forget you, Ms. Green."

The Assistant Principal was there. SGT Bear thanked him with a salute. The Principal was there. SGT Bear acknowledged him graciously.

While shaking hands with SGT Bear, the Principal said, "SGT Bear, after you settle in and rest, the school wants to give you a Welcome Home Party. I want to have several dignitaries join us, as well."

SGT Bear smiled but said nothing. Frankly, he dreaded crowds and parties, and he just wanted to stay home, and do nothing. It would be a long time, he thought, before he would ever want to face a large crowd of people.

11

HOME

"Hello, Dr. Brown. This is Chaplain Walker on the phone. How are you, my friend?"

"I'm all right, Dr. Walker. Are you calling from Afghanistan?"

"We've just arrived at Langley Air Force Base. You are the first person I've called. We got here ahead of schedule, so most of the families have not yet arrived."

"It's good to hear your voice. You sound good on the phone. Is everything okay?" asked Dr. Brown.

"Yes," said Dr. Walker, "thanks to the good Lord, I'm safe and sound, but I have a favor to ask."

"What can I do?"

"How soon could you see SGT Bear, a Soldier I am very fond of?"

Dr. Brown replied, "Is today too early, my friend?"

"May I come with him, and also bring SGT Bear's wife and son?"

"Too easy," replied Dr. Brown. "Can we meet at noon in my office?" asked Dr. Brown. It was the only opening in his schedule

"That will work."

"Chaplain Walker, I almost forgot. SGT Bear should come to Behavioral Health at 1130 to complete his registration, and take the BHDP."

"Will do, Dr. Brown, but what is the BHDP?"

"The BHDP is the Behavioral Health Data Platform. His answers to the questions will help me understand his psychological functioning. Embedded in the survey is an important battery of psychological tests. I'll review the results with him."

SGT Bear and his Family meet Dr. Brown

"Lady Bear, SGT Bear, and Little Bear, and Chaplain Walker, I am so pleased to have the honor of meeting you today. I respect military families. Our country owes so much to you. Thank you, SGT Bear, and thank you to the entire Bear Family for serving our country," said Dr. Brown.

Chaplain Walker cleared his throat.

"What is it, Chaplain Walker?" asked Dr. Brown.

"I'm sorry, Dr. Brown, but we arrived late, and SGT Bear had no time to complete the BHDP. Can he do that next time?"

"If there is a next time," SGT Bear said with a suggestion of anger in his voice.

"SGT Bear," said the Chaplain firmly, "I gave my word to the psychiatrist in Kandahar that you would receive the care you need."

"Your word, Chaplain Walker, is your word. My word is my word.

Dr. Brown is a stranger to me. Who is he? What does he know about me? What does he know about the Army? Has Dr. Brown ever been deployed?"

SGT Bear's right leg started moving up and down rapidly. Rapid leg movement is a sign commonly seen in PTSD. Anger shaped his face, tightening his jaw muscles, widening his eyes, and deepening the furrows in his forehead between his eyebrows. He was breathing very rapidly.

Lady Bear moved her chair closer to him. She put her arm around his neck. With her left hand, she softly patted the back of his hand. Hardly audible, she whispered, "Honey, I love you."

Little Bear was afraid. He had never seen his dad this way.

Dr. Brown spoke with a smile in his voice. "Chaplain Walker, what the SGT just said makes a lot of sense. He is exactly correct. I am a total stranger to him. He does not know me from Adam. Shall we all go to the PX-TRA, get a pizza, and call it a day?"

"Pizza is a splendid idea, Dr. Brown, but not today," said the Chaplain.

"I want the Bears to get to know you, Dr. Brown."

Who is Dr. Brown?

"Let me apologize to you first, Dr. Brown. I do not want to embarrass you, and I don't want to make you sound like a superman, but SGT Bear and his family need to know who you are.

I can tell them who you are because once I was under your care for PTSD.

I didn't want to be here as a patient, either.

I came first under false pretenses. I came to you, Dr. Brown, asking for advice on dealing with my laundry man's son. He was hooked on drugs.

When I came back, I was fearful of humbling myself to another man. It made me feel weak, but Dr. Brown you encouraged me to feel healthy again.

I have PTSD from combat. I was also in the Pentagon when the terrorist hijacked an American Airlines jetliner and crashed it into the building. The attack killed several of my friends. It was the same day the terrorists demolished the Twin Towers with two other hijacked jetliners."

Little Bear remembered what his dad had told his class about the dark cloud over the Twin Towers. Nobody notice, but Little Bear shuttered and moved closer to his mother.

"It took time and patience, but Dr. Brown helped me understand and manage my PTSD."

SGT Bear's leg stopped moving rapidly up and down. He was listening.

"Who is this person we call Dr. Brown? It's a real good question, SGT Bear.

Look at the wall behind his seat, but first look at him.

Dr. Brown has sat in that chair for the past eleven years. He has treated thousands of Soldiers with PTSD.

Why does he do it?

Is it only a job?

He does what he does because he will tell you, he felt called by God to leave his private practice, and leave his family, and his friends in Charlottesville to come to Fort Lee to "help win the war by helping Soldiers."

Notice three University of Virginia degrees on his wall. There is no room up there for his fourth University of

Virginia degree.

Notice the Legion of Merit awarded to Dr. Brown at Walter Reed Army Medical Center.

Has COL Brown ever been deployed? He traveled in his mind and his heart with each Soldier he treated. Every battle described to him became real as if he too were in the convoy, on the mission, and personally witnessed hundreds of Roll Calls.

Does Dr. Brown have PTSD? You can bet on it. No one can actively listen to the horrors of combat for eleven years and remain untouched, unaffected by it.

SGT Bear, meet Dr. Brown."

SGT Bear stood up, saluted Dr. Brown, and firmly shook his hand. The two men embraced. It was the end of the first of many sessions.

Welcome Home Party

SGT Bear, like all Soldiers with PTSD, does not like surprises. He kept asking Little Bear, "When is your class party? Will it be the last party?"

Little Bear is learning about PTSD from Dr. Brown's website, sacredgroundmedia.com. He patiently answered his dad.

"I will bring home the notice from school today, dad. It

will have all the information we need to know."

"Will it be like the party last year, Little Bear?"

"That party will never happen again, dad. Most of it was surprising to all of us. We had no idea what would happen next.

Ms. Green said this party must be quiet and dignified. There will be no surprises, dad. I promise you."

"Will I have to give a speech or anything like that?"

"No," said Little Bear. "No speeches by you. Nothing like that is required, dad. I give you my word."

"Who will be there, Little Bear?"

"Ms. Green has invited the Assistant Principal and the Principal, and a "mystery guest," but everybody knows it's our Congressman. Yes, I'll be there; I believe that is it, dad," said Little Bear.

"I want to bring Chaplain Walker with me. Will that be all right?"

"This is your party, dad. You can bring anyone you wish to bring."

The Big Day

The school auditorium was packed.

Ms. Green's class sat in the middle section in the front seats.

The Principal led the Pledge of Allegiance to the American flag. The pledge was permitted only on special occasions.

The school band played God Bless America.

The students applauded loudly as SGT and Lady Bear marched in. He wore his dress blue uniform; Lady Bear wore a new, yellow dress.

Behind the Bears, Chaplain and Mrs. Walker marched proudly, both smiling.

Behind the Walkers, came Congressman Randy Forbes and his friend, Senator Paul A. Trible. Senator Trible from the honorable Commonwealth of Virginia is now the President of Christopher Newport University.

The Ceremony

"Ladies and gentlemen, honored guests, SGT and Mrs. Bear, please bow your heads for a moment of silence and a prayer led by Congressman Randy Forbes."

An unusually quiet moment swept over the school auditorium.

Randy Forbes prayed.

"Before I pray," he said, "I want you to know that every week that I am in Washington, a group of congressmen join me in earnest prayer for our nation."

His words and his thoughts went directly to Heaven.

"Before I take my seat, I want you to meet Senator Trible. He was my inspiration to become a congressman."

Senator Trible, a humble man of few words, came to the microphone.

"We are blessed with freedom in America because people like SGT Bear are willing to leave their families to fight to keep our freedom. Thank you, SGT Bear. Thank you, Lady Bear."

Little Bear and Tommy

"Little Bear and Tommy, will you come to the front, please?"

The boys were shocked but excited. They came to the stage as fast as possible.

"I heard what you two young men did to help SGT and Lady Bear. Thank you.

Ms. Green, will you come to the stage?"

Ms. Green, unprepared for this, could hardly move.

Tommy and Little Bear went to Ms. Green's seat. Each took one of her hands and escorted her to the stage.

Congressman Forbes joined Senator Trible. He spoke into the microphone.

"We have been authorized by the Congress of the United States of America to announce that Ms. Green, her entire class, this school's Assistant Principal and Principal will be awarded the Congressional Citizens Freedom Medal on the 15th of the next month."

The audience roared its approval loudly but respectfully.

The Principal came to the microphone and tried to calm down the students. It was no easy task.

Finally, after five or even ten minutes, the Principal gave up. He could hold his arms up no longer, so he waited until the audience decided to stop applauding. Sternly, the Principal said, "We must not forget the reason we are here today. Ladies and gentlemen, let me present our school hero, SGT Bear."

If the earlier applause seemed endless, this was longer and louder.

SGT Bear

SGT Bear stood silently at the microphone. He would rather have been in Afghanistan or Iraq. He was briefly distracted by worrisome and painful memories of the war racing through his mind.

When the noise lessened and finally stopped, SGT Bear

spoke.

"I am not a hero. I only did what any Soldier would do. Please don't call me a hero, please. I'm just a Soldier."

A chant broke out among the students. "SGT Bear was there. SGT Bear was there."

Over and over, "SGT Bear was there. SGT Bear was there."

Soon everyone was chanting, including the dignitaries on the stage. "SGT Bear was there. SGT Bear was there. SGT Bear was there."

SGT Bear's silence turned into a smile.

When the chanting stopped, SGT Bear said, "Thank you. I guess everyone needs a hero."

One of SGT Bear's Heroes

"I want you to meet one of my heroes, COL James Edward Walker."

Chaplain Walker joined SGT Bear at the microphone.

"Chaplain Walker," said SGT Bear, "tell these people what a chaplain does in combat."

"A chaplain lives among the Soldiers in the fighting to get to know them.

The chaplain is the only representative and reminder of

God's presence in war.

The chaplain conducts worship services, performs counseling, and, unfortunately, he or she holds funerals and memorial services.

The chaplain helps Soldiers deal with the ugliness of war and death.

The chaplain is a spiritual advisor to leaders and commanders in combat."

A hush fell over the auditorium.

The chaplain informed students about the importance of spiritual leadership to Soldiers during combat and the human cost of war.

SGT Bear and Chaplain Walker took their seats.

A Good but Unexpected Announcement

Congressman Forbes came to the microphone.

"SGT Bear," he said, "please come forward.

You told me you are not a hero. Would it surprise you to learn that many people disagree with you?"

"Yes, it would surprise me, Sir. I just did my job. I did nothing more. I tried not to do anything bad, Sir."

"Let me tell you who disagrees with you, SGT Bear.

Your Company Commander disagrees.

Your Battalion Commander disagrees.

Your Brigade Commander disagrees.

The Department of Defense ordered that you receive the Silver Star Medal, the third-highest ranking military award for valor, for your heroic conduct in Kandahar, Afghanistan.

Congratulations, SGT Bear, Lady Bear, and Little Bear.

God has indeed blessed America with good Soldiers like you, and with good families like yours. May your journey back here today be a living testimony that all our citizens highly value you and your family."

Everyone stood and applauded.

Everyone chanted, "SGT Bear is here! But SGT Bear was there!" "SGT Bear is here!" "But SGT Bear was there."

The Welcome Home Party for SGT Bear never really ended. It lasted in the mind of everyone who attended.

The chant for SGT Bear never really ended. It played melodically in the mind of everyone who attended.

12

CHLOE

As the Welcome Home Celebrations concluded, everybody wanted to shake SGT Bear's hand, pat him on the back, or just say thank you.

All he could do was smile.

Everyone thanked Lady Bear and Little Bear in the same way.

Tommy and Betty were smiling.

From behind, a girl's hand tugged on SGT Bear's dress blues jacket.

It was Chloe.

SGT Bear kneeled down, hugged Chloe tightly, and said, "I thought of you every day, Chloe. I felt your prayers and the prayers of your church.

I also prayed for your dad, Chloe.

God answered your prayer, and God answered my prayer.

I found your dad in Afghanistan. He's a very brave Soldier. We became friends. I told him about your prayer requests in the Hopewell Baptist Church."

Chloe's eyes sparkled with real joy.

"I knew God would hear our prayer. Where is my dad?" she pleaded.

"He called your mother from Afghanistan and begged for her forgiveness. His PTSD is responding to treatment.

Your mother believes in second chances.

Your dad and mother are standing right behind you."

Chloe ran to her father and jumped into his outstretched arms.

Tommy was there, too.

Chloe Speaks

"And this is what happened when I requested prayer, and the people prayed," Chloe said to her dad.

Chloe spoke out loud to her dad so others could hear and believe: "God answered prayers.

We show our love for God by keeping His commandments.

We show our love for each other by loving them enough to pray for them.

God's greatest commandment is to love Him with all our heart, mind, and soul, and to love our neighbor as ourselves."

Those standing nearest to Chloe said they saw tears of joy flow from the eyes of Chloe and her dad during their wonderful reunion.

Understanding the Need to have Things Just Right

Tommy said, "Finally, the need to have everything just right is beginning to make sense to me. I never knew it might be a symptom of combat PTSD."

Chloe asked, "Goldilocks ran away when awakened from sleep in the bed of one of the Three Bears. Does that mean she had PTSD?

In the story of the Three Bears, Goldilocks wanted to have things just right, but does it mean she had PTSD?"

Chaplain Walker, standing nearby, answered Chloe's questions.

"Sometimes wanting to have things just right may mean caring and hoping that something special we are doing for someone turns out well.

Unfortunately, too often the desire for things to be just right is little more than being selfish.

People who are perfectionists struggle all the time with needing things just right.

When is having things just right the best course of action?" he asked.

I believe that having things just right is best when it shows the most love for someone else.

Try not to misunderstand the difference between "having one's way" and the need to have everything "just right."

Too often Soldiers with PTSD are perceived as "always wanting to have things their way." That perception leads to resentment and anger.

Soldiers with PTSD may be unaware of their need to have things just right.

It takes understanding and a loving family to tolerate apparent self-centeredness while PTSD treatment is helping heal the injured mind.

Perfected caring often means helping arrange the circumstances for others to have a life that is good, but it doesn't have to be just right."

Chloe's Example

The ceremony was over.

Most of the students had returned to their classrooms, but a few students and guests remained in the auditorium.

Chloe's family and Little Bear's family, relaxed and thankful, gathered for a few minutes. They listened carefully to Chaplain Walker as he continued to speak softly to them.

Ms. Green was there.

Dorothy Ann was there.

The assistant principal was there.

The principal was there.

The lunch room staff was there.

Even the SWAT Team was there.

"Chloe shows us the only way to have a life that is good, but it is not always "just right," the chaplain said.

"Chloe is on a first-name basis with Jesus. He is the One whom she loves.

Chloe stays in very close touch with Jesus through prayer and Bible study. Chloe wants to have a relationship that is just right with Jesus."

Everyone understood the chaplain's words of wisdom.

Everyone was immediately comforted.

Time froze. It was like a DVD on pause.

The long period of silence was healing.

Tommy said, "I feel great.

Little Bear, will you go fishing with me today after school?"

The question surprised Little Bear. "Fishing was the last

thing on my mind," he said.

Somehow, the way Little Bear appeared and the way he spoke seemed funny.

Everybody laughed.

Dorothy Ann came to the rescue. "I have a better idea. Tommy, Little Bear and I will meet at the mall after school and have our first Bible study. Chloe can also come."

Chloe smiled and said, "Thanks, but I'm going to the library. Tommy can walk me there after school. You can all study the Bible, and I can read what others may have written about the Three Bears after Goldilocks ran away. Tommy can tell you all about my version of the ending."

Everyone was happy, truly happy.

Terror has touched many more than two Army families, but God touched these two Army families and continued to bless them abundantly.